ARQTIQ

ARQTIQ

ANNA ADOLPH

ISBN: 978-93-5420-643-6

Published: 1899

LECTOR HOUSE LLP
E-MAIL: lectorpublishing@gmail.com

ARQTIQ
A STUDY OF THE MARVELS AT THE NORTH POLE

BY

MRS. ANNA ADOLPH

1899

ARQTIQ.

I

Saying "I will go with thee
To yon isles of mystery."

Always fond of the marvelous, I conceived a strong desire to go to the North Pole.

To obviate the dangers of the trip I invented a coach, that was also ship and balloon. Its silken canopy is inflatable to strong wings or wide sails. Its wheels are wide rimmed, to glide over snow, and paneled for water paddles. When it is finished and stored I select some friends to accompany me. My most personal loved ones. A volatile fair-haired gent—my husband, and a fair-haired little maiden friend, sit on the front seat. On the back seat are sitting my aged father and myself, our black eyes snapping with expectation.

Waving my hands to the few gathered to see us off, I say: "This undertaking is of desire to gain knowledge. Success, surmounting all obstacles will take us to the summit of the round earth, where, ages past as ages future will accord us first record."

Charley turns levers to start, as little Mae's mamma says: "You will be the Mascot, Mae Searles. But I do not think you will go very far," dubiously.

"You will change your mind, mamma, when I bring you home a little bear," makes us laugh.

"I will be glad to get you for my little bear."

"All the rest of us," I answered, "will take care of her."

"No doubt," she replies, "as far as you go in your odd rig," facetiously.

Our wheels turn slowly and silently. Then with a low tinkling of the strain, "Good Bye, Sweet Heart," Mae had slipped her music box in one, wound to that harmony.

We are Californians and take the C. P. railroad for our eastward route, our wheels being grooved to fit the track. Speeding merrily, we give vent to our imaginations of coming events.

"Will there really be a pole, Auntie?"

"That is for us to find out, dear. I sometimes think there is a stem there covered with ice, that holds the earth to an apple planet tree."

"But the astronomers would have seen the tree," argues my father.

"They could not look so far. Only as far as the other star apples. May not the Milky Way be a branch?" I suggest.

We now become aware that a train is approaching on the single track that is hanging over the grade on the canyon side. We have no choice but to unfurl our wings and rise in the air, as the engineer wildly blows his whistle. Brushing the pine tree tops, we cross over the peak and seek the track on the other side of it, selecting an opening in a thicket for that purpose.

Finding it occupied by miners digging away, we hallo, when they look every way but up, as we land in their midst as though dropped from the sky. Their consternation is depicted in set jaws, as we give military salute and roll off.

This feat, so skilfully accomplished, denotes an expert hand in our motorman, who had been practicing faithfully, as a bird to fly, a swimmer or cyclist. As exhilarant to him as to us, and much lessened our distance, causes Mae to clap her hands and ask, "Why not fly all the time?"

"We want to save that force until we have more serious need," Charley replies. "I hope that poor boy who fell over the log while eating his breakfast and ran away, will recover and go back," makes us all laugh uproariously, when zipp! whir-r!! over we go and lay on our side, the wheels still revolving.

The grade just here, level from the ground excavated by the miners, saved us from a serious mishap. To have rolled to the Canyon River would have damaged us greatly. As it is we cannot recover the track without that descent. So we twist our car upright (we are fastened in our seats), square it to the hill and down we go, losing our breath as we plump splashing into the water.

Our bonny wheels take paddle stroke and carry us, laughing over, and up the opposite bank to the track there, in its sinuous course.

"We laughed too quick," says father. "That friend at whom we laughed dropped that fork on the rail. I see him behind that boulder."

We leave the narrow-gauge track at its terminus without stopping, and have no other special accident in this vicinity.

The sun has chased frost and rose hues the higher snow peaks. Sierra Nevada (snowy) in its most interesting locality is around. Having come on the narrow-gauge railroad that connects the two largest and oldest of the mining cities with the broad-gauge of the Central Pacific, we are rounding out on the latter over the famous Cape Horn. Spring is in her first freshness. We sniff its fragrance, as we shall continue to do, following its pioneer march until our arrival at our destination to enjoy our summer at the pole, where it is most enjoyable and the only tolerable season. From apparently bare ground are flying the cyclamen banners of the johnny-jump-up. The blue sage (sun dial) gives a lake of national colors, interspersed with the scarlet of the gorgeous fireweed, whose leaves and blossoms glow alike. Mae gleefully reaches to a dogwood lily (artist's favorite), then snatches a tuft of pink primrose that covers a bank and decorates its edge, while I cook the breakfast upon our steam heater. It is so late I make it serve for dinner also. Putting omelette and ripe strawberries beside the spinach and wild duck. As I finish Mae emits a long whistle, as a red-breasted linnet—the first—flies close to us to get our sweet food company, then sings, to earn it and call its family.

The chapparal is faintly green. But the manzanita—sung of poets, or ought to be—in its immaculate green leaves adorning the winter, with red stems of eternal beauty, is covered with pink waxen sprays, as fragrant, as it is like, the lily of the valley. A momentary regret comes to leave in California this worshipped shrub. Its blossoms develop to little green-apple fruit, the size of peas, of edible flavor. Manzanita is the Indian name for little apple.

Charley appreciates my feelings as he calls out, "Take a last look," when father, to turn the tide, passes the muffins. Our glance down the mountain side falls upon a ranch, tiny in the depths; a maid of midget size throws invisible corn to mice-size chickens that flock around; Charley hurls deftly a cracker toward them that falls far short upon the mountain side. My spirits rise. To be here sings a grateful pæan in my breast. To write it is not half the story.

I remember lovingly the sister cities left behind. Mining born and golden reared, with their Californian continual lawns, social halls and grand hotels for the floating population, this last much improved by the efforts of the Salvation Army, who have charmed the crowd to good behavior as they enjoy appreciatively their sweet-voiced pleadings.

I look out at the country, dotted with quartz-mill chimneys, with their heavy roar, as the heavy stamp crushes the granite to free the gold imprisoned in their bastille. To all we bid good-bye, as we turn Cape Horn, and though still among the clouds, we see and hear the rushing river below. As all streams here are given to chatty hilarity, I think once more of the one where oft I have walked on trailed path.

I muse on until in time we salute the desert plain, with its sage brush and dog cities. Stations are not hailed by us (as in time a small crowd awaits us). Silently we appear; like a shadow disappear.

Our seats are so constructed that we can stand and exercise, rock or lie down at ease. Partaking our meals without alighting, we have no occasion to lose time. Our casing open, banners flying. I have brought handwork and books. Father is carving on some queer rotary wheel that gives three separate motions. Charley and Mae, on the seat in front, amuse each other and call us to the special sights.

Chicago! We leisurely arrive and traverse silently, street after street, sadly impressed that the continuous magnificence in equality of buildings, found nowhere else, was dearly bought.

Citizens are crowding our path; obstructing our progress by their progressive ardor, for some one has telegraphed them of our intended exploration; to our unexpected aspirations, unheeding our desires, they hurrah lustily for our success.

Thanking them, we start on, grateful in our hearts for their sympathy. We do not stop in any other city, even passing over the suspension bridge quite silently, though lost in ecstasy at its cataract view.

Evading detention in New York, we whirl over the Brooklyn Bridge without minding the many curious gazers.

Arriving at Coney Island beach, though a storm is coming on, we light our interior and in the dusk are about to drop into the sea. A shout goes up outside and strong hands hold us. Near us is a carriage whose horses we had frightened. In it is an aged man of martial bearing, who recognizes my father.

"Oh, it is *you*, is it, meandering at night like a firebug. Turn around now and go home with me," he said, cordially.

"Haven't time; we are bound to the North Pole." Hurrying up so quickly, we break away and sink beneath the toppling waves.

Pelted and tossed all night we welcome daylight; but flash, crack, roar, we draw ourselves closer together, and sink in the depths beneath the turmoil, to find other disturbance. A massed army of swordfish hold battle-front with glowing eyes to an opposing array of giant whales, who ponderously coming, lash the sea into a vortex.

The two columns colliding, the first leap in white streaks, curl, and land on the latter's backs, dip and dye their swords. The whales shake them off and beat them to death in myriads, to be followed by myriads more, until the sea is red, when suddenly the cavalry swords fly, disappearing in the distance.

The victorious artillery, the whales, blow themselves, weariedly. We go closer to them—too close—as they are a warrior band. A big general opens his mouth towards us, disconcerting to our stomachs; we beat a hasty retreat to a safe distance, where we watch the camp followers, a jumbling mass of veritable sea monsters.

When all is quiet we rise to the surface, to find it quiet there, too. The sun shining brightly on an iceberg, whose edge, sending up a few whale spouts, resolves it into a fountainous white island.

I muse aloud! "Does the under war cause the upper war, or *vice versa*? What is war? Ocean's elements and life as restless as man. Plant-life and rocks, also, struggle and upheave. Why is war? Resulting only to change. God's evolution but a program of variety." I study it thus, in inspiration, hoping it leads to fore-destined improvement.

I am hearing the word Arbitration. "Oh, yes, papa; when arbitration stops men's wars, will the elements follow, and what then?"

II

"Those starry choirs that watch around the pole."

—Casimir.

The first iceberg is but the precursor of many that block our way. Then block the land to perpetual imprisonment. Giving us first taste of this specialty of our trip. As we stop a few days in the last place of civilization.

We find good entertainment with pleasant people who are willing to aid us in our endeavor for knowledge, yet solemnly warn us not to dare the dangers ahead. They stock us with dried meat; supply us with double sealskin outfits; in fact, sealskins line our sleigh to aid in keeping us warm. They end by giving us their uttermost paths.

Had our home friends in California been more solicitous, and amused themselves less at our expense, at this juncture we would have returned to them, for our hearts are dropping like lead. But our pride aids us, as our eyes bravely scan the pole star ahead.

"Mae, do you want to go home?" as I see her wipe the tears out of her big blue eyes.

"Not I; this is the best part of it. Only the frosty air makes me cry."

"Do you not want to see your mamma?"

"Yes, but I will have so much more to tell her," waking to enthusiasm and paramount faith.

Polished ice-glass in hand I firmly wave adieu.

In the last few days of our stay have been finished preparations for what, to the nation, is a centennial celebration. A barbecue is held on an ice glittering plaza. Emerald ice tables, chamois-clothed, hold a wondrous feast. Whole reindeer rigs, the sledge a pastry; great Christmas trees are confections. This now engages the crowds.

We rub our hands together, and, shall I say it, our noses, in local fashion of "good bye," as our prow points north.

We have carefully selected this season of the year, with intent to follow the continual dawn light—night and day—of this region, which yet faint, is hardly sufficient to keep us moving swiftly, when, lo, near us darts up a bright glare, followed by others, around and ahead, as far as we can see, illumining the air. They are bonfires of the celebration. Heaps of cones, added to yearly, surround a ring of pine trees, the center a tall, hollow trunk as chimney. The gorgeous flickering of glory, I feel to believe, is miles in extent.

Climbing miles up the heavy atmosphere, it is advanced to iceberg peaks, beyond and below the horizon. Visited thus only for ages, do they inclose the pole? Are they the goal we seek? Springing up the crystal shafts in warmth of welcome are reflected back again and beckon us on.

Our minds in sublime mood, to silence, are disturbed, as father suddenly jerks up his head. "It is the red fire of the north." The rare mystery the superstitious ancients believed to be a sign of war is now solved, and the simple in fact is most beautiful of sight.

Our path is strangely smooth, as though some hitherto sea had congealed and left a frozen plain, which gives us grateful relief until our direction ceases and the last marked path stops, and an icy lobe rears high before us.

Clamp-spurring our wheels we climb its height, to find a table formation, level graded, an unmistakable sign of ice-locked land, as if an island included in the cold grasp that holds the sea. We do not go far, when a pile of ice rocks hem in a space. We proceed to inspect. Hastily curving by, we are suddenly brushed by a bush, and berries rattle lusciously on our window-pane. Flinging it open a balmy air salutes us, forcing us out upon a bright-hued snow-flower carpet.

"What, berries in spring! in Arctic forcing-houses! no cold night to delay matters!" as Charley is about to cram his mouth. But I, on closely examining, fail to identify them, and jot in my book a new name, "Onigogies." He looks over to read. "Gogies, gogies, gorge us, please."

"Tu whu a whu," wavers our brains and quivers our eyes, as we see a great white owl perched on our banner, blinking. I see near by an apple vine. I reach out and take a most beautiful red specimen, before I am aware that it is already in the mouth of a serpent, coiled around the twig. Unconsciously an Eve, as unconscious, also, is the reptile, who looks at me with kind, appreciative eyes. But I drop the apple and get into the sleigh, quite weak, unable to prevent Mae from taking and eating another, giving one to father. Seeing me in, Charley gets ready to enter, by loading the bottom. The owl has gone, but approaching is a gorgeous stork of orange plumage. Of camel size, it coolly steps over us, as the rest quickly step in and we move forward.

Thinking this may be a lost Eden, I look curiously to discover the life tree, to see Mae and father, who have turned deathly pale, reel in their seats. Stopping quickly, we put snow on their heads and bind it by leaves of a high shrub we are under. Shuddering, they grasp the leaves in their teeth and swallow the juice as their breath revives. A red glow on their cheeks. Was it the leaves of healing? Much trampled beneath had given us roadway. As expected, we enter a herd of foxes, who are barking in play and basking in the unusual light; as all else, unnoticing us, we glide along quite securely.

Charley has studied the lesson of the apple, as he audaciously reaches down and takes one, and calmly eats it in conjunction with the leaves, to my perturbed attention.

We reach the edge of the island and go down to the sea plain again, which is here more rough in icy waves, making the travel quite difficult. The waves grew larger until mountains high, then lessen and gradually disappear, having unfolded to us a frozen storm at sea.

The surface is smoother and smoother; so that we start up swiftly. A gale scurries toward us from behind. As it strikes us Charley opens valves and we all rise in our seats, unable to contain our ardor, as miles are covered in our exceeding speed, which continues as the moments and hours pass, father's speed-measure marking a mile a second. Hundreds of miles are covered and the ice is still smooth. Knowing we are not so far away from the peaks that point the pole, we hourly anticipate a view as of masts arising at sea, but instead, we are shocked to see the flame-hued sky settle densely in a fog. So long our friend, its warmth had melted the congealed air and now clouds our nautical bearings. Our compass is our sole northly guide. But what—what is the matter with it that it hangs its head and stops? We are lost!

In frenzy, now, the hours go by as we circle blindly, when a luminant point attracts us far away. Is it the serried guide shaft? It is.

Famished and cold—our steam spent and wheels broken—we make but slow speed toward the flickering gleam. Attaining it, we have only left us our wings, by which we rise up the cliff side of the topping pinnacle—to see others, massed in braided and arcaded confusion before us. Weakening, while above their splintering and crashing avalanches, we drop on the side of the sheerest bayonet of all, as hundreds of hues are changing and ranging in glistening sea waves in a deep, long valley below us. Not long, but a round level plain, girdled by this ring of bergs that hem it in.

Our pained eyes watch father stolidly take our local bearings, then with him shout in audible voice: "The North Pole!"

III

"Lead, kindly, light!
Lead thou me on."

The north star in the heavens, shining faintly through the half-clear atmosphere, has decided us on our locality at the dearly attained goal, costing us friends, and country, and possibly our lives.

The sound of our voices falls dead around and echoes into the deep valley below. No sign of the beautiful city we had fancifully pictured. Thankful to die in the light, with the stars to take our last breath, is only left us.

Mae complainingly whimpers: "There isn't a pole at all!"

"Nor open sea," growls Charley, hoarsely.

"The width of the valley determines the flattening of the earth, though," sighs father.

Fall dead around, did I say? our voice—I level the glass down the berg side beneath me. I see at the sound a snowy mass turn about, with a human face uplifted toward me.

So great the size and wondrous fair the countenance I believed myself deceived, as it quickly turns back. But I see two hands clasp together in signal. Then low organ notes swell from below, which, when loudest grown, suddenly stop.

When the sun in hailing gleam lights a tall spire, supporting a ring of gold points arising from the valley center, which I now trace for the first time. Led to examine the valley around it, I see shapes of domes and wall—signs of a buried city. What are they doing? Whirling and shaking? Presto! the snow canvas rolls off, unveiling a full-fledged and much-alive city to my amazed mind. From last extreme of despair my hopes suddenly arise to so sudden height! I fall forward and cover my eyes, to keep my brain intact. The city at last. City of Zion! Sung of poets and portrayed of artists inspired of its contour and elysian beauty. Hope raises a hosanna in my breast that is chorused around me, where I now give my attention.

The human presence below, with feather-plume robes, so like snow, swaying back, is hastening up in giant strides, anxious expectation on his face. As he reaches the ledge on which we lodge the choral voices around disclose a throng of people similar to him lining all the mountain sides. Their pæan of praise to their city's prowess ended, with shouts and conversation they prepare to descend. Nearly running over us, babes to them in size, they at last spy us, as the first kneels in adoration, his hands over us in protection and token of possession.

With tender emotion he essays to quiet our alarm, managing at last to emit words that sounded like "Welcome, Unions!" For a moment I wonder if other Americans are here lost before us. Then we bow low in reply. Assured of our trust in him he takes charge and lifts us from our ruined vehicle to another, standing near, which is no less than a great white albatross, one of many now being mounted by the throng. Robes are drawn about us, after we are presented to a lady, also in his charge, who, with less success, attempts the words he first used. Feeling quite among friends, as he lifts a feather-tufted guiding wand resting on the bird's head, I turn to the lady by my side, whose first glance, as though in bitterness, before our arrival, has changed to liveliest sociability in gestures, nods and smiles upon Mae, who is cuddled in her lap.

With womanly curiosity I essay to learn the city's name. Understanding my desire she essayed to reply, in cordial, harmonious tones, "Arc." Farther inquiry in my eyes, I get the farther delineation, "It circles Aurora," meaning, no doubt, the electric centre. Content with this, I scan the dimensions growing, as we approach, and ride high above, the snowy pinions of the bird throng clouding the air.

Courts are numerous, covered with great glass domes and domes rolled back. As we turn down to one of these I hear father whisper to our host, "How do you know English?"

With effort he kindly gives the following: "My father, when younger, explored a great deal upon the iceberg sea around. Venturing too far one day, he became lost in an island garden, to find camped there a people like you, who fed and cared for him." How simple; his kindness is in gratitude.

"But where are the people?" father farther inquired.

"I do not know. He became lost again from them to find his own city."

Alighting, we are led through conservatory halls to an apartment-like hall. Of great magnificence, it is yet quite homelike, with great cushions strewn about that are seats for the great people but beds in size for us. I fall on one and am soon fast asleep. Awaking partially, a melody is soothing my senses. Sitting up, I see a fountain whence issues the sounds. In it I bathe face and hands, when the water, acting medicinal, I feel revived and buoyant, also quite hungry. Father and Charley are talking, the latter ending with "It suits me."

Mae, still asleep, talks spasmodically. "Oh, auntie! Oh, mamma!" At the last a pain enters my heart, never more to leave. Opening her eyes, she slowly takes in the situation. Seeing the pain in my face, she throws her arms about my neck and says, gently, "No matter, auntie; it is a sweet place here, anyway."

The rest now giving way to hunger, as our hosts duly regard us with infantile solicitude, I put my hand in my mouth, as in the latter's fashion. Immediately wheels of itself into the room a table laden with food. Staring at its wizard-like action, we are seated to it. No dish, knife or fork, or board. Probably not in the land. An enameled lily leaf. The food, light and solid, piled in little fruit cups. One is put in each our mouths, cup and all. I taste and find it palatable. Our appetites satisfied, out wheels the table, making Mae smile and become merry. Seeing us still high perched, our jolly friends rally around us, pull our toes and pinch our cheeks, until I wish I had refrained in initiating this program. Soon in comes a hassock and wheeling to us, gives us an opportunity to alight. Mae down last, remains seated on it, when it starts around the room with her, pirouetting in mazy figures, giving its occupant mazy face.

When stopped, the host whistles, to bring from a corner two great white mice, kitten size. As he twirls his fingers, they fall to the floor, a green sward; folding their four pink paws to their breasts, they become round balls, thus roll about, greatly to our amusement.

This has suggested to the lady, who proposes to "go out in town to an entertainment that is funny, oh, so funny."

The host, in gleesome impulse, elects to take me. Raising me on his hand, he asks my name. Charley, quite diverted, gives it, "Anna."

"Ah, you are angel, Anna!" when Charley reads the puzzle, remarking, "He means 'English.'" Then he kisses me squarely in the mouth, to my immediate struggle to get down, which I succeed in doing while he is taking Charley in his other hand, who now, unlike other husbands, proceeds to lecture me. "Do not be odd; you see it is all right. It is evening hour in America (swallowing); we will enjoy this, our first evening here."

Mae, who has taken to the hand I have left, reaches and pinches him; at which I laugh and spring into a pocket in front of the lady, upon whose shoulder sits my father, his hand holding her feather cap. So utterly without matronly dignity am I, I am glad for once that home friends cannot see my position.

Getting into the center of the street, she stops, (I nearly fall) and sits upon a chair, raised from the road-bed by the man, who takes another. The object is plain, when we move swiftly along as on a track.

Mae asks ingenuously her bearer's name; he gives it in Arc language, what sounds to us like "Show Off," which we shall now call him. Then looking to my bearer he says: "She is Aunt Robet, a dear old maid, who is always taking care of us, papa and I, when mother is away." He goes over and squeezes her shoulders. As father innocently sticks a pin into his hand, he looks so queerly at the hurt, it is plain he does not know the cause, or never felt the like before. In our childish role we still question: "Where is your papa?" "Oh, he is always in his house (room). You can live with him," looking at my father. Seeing us unwilling at such an arrangement, his aunt explains: "He is a student, a very great savant, who is always busy in his office or study." This alters the matter; father's eyes glisten with expectation.

Arrived at the hall I see a great space in the floor, that is grooved in pattern. I look to see if a cable line is drawing through, when I am deposited on a chair directly above. The rest have chairs near by. Mae retaining her place in Show Off's lap. The other chairs in the room are being rapidly filled. I cannot determine the entertainment so wait developments. Not long. The word is given, the chairs start off, getting a swift gait. I suddenly remember Mae's hassock, but she is watching Charley, who takes a firm hold, as the important look, assumed at our departure, goes slowly off his face, ejaculating but once "Shake." I think, too, shake, for quiver, jerk, jump, all in rotation; music playing is the order. Enjoying our mutual discomfiture, our chairs opposite, we are treated at the last to a grand bounce, that sends us into each other's arms, so close. Had not Mae been held firm, she would have fallen, in her convulsion of mirth.

We lose no time in getting down, and close to our bearers. Aunt Robet, placid in demeanor, I calculate how to get even with her. Though she had declared it funny, I look at her viciously, when she condescends to graciously explain: "This is our outing celebration; the city shakes off its veil to greet the sun; shaking is, therefore, the order of the day." Hence this little exercise, I was happy to have amused her.

We ride now leisurely home, viewing the heavy buildings of great blocks of ice, shining in the sunlight. Why they do not melt I cannot tell. Afterwards I learn they are covered with an enamel that preserves them. The picturing on their sides is done by fracturing; the graceful cornices and other trimmings are in imitation of snowflake crystals, relieving to beauty their solidity. Quite exhausted on our return, we are given apartments to ourselves, in which we prepare to rest.

Convinced that false positions are unfortunate, I resolve to adopt a dignified bearing, suitable to my maturity, my short experience in babyhood, however remunerative, proving quite objectionable in excess of bestowment.

Hearing father sigh, as he watches the dawn that beckons to arise instead of sleep, I essay to comfort him. "Dear father, has not God sent us here to convert them?" "Too intelligent," he mutters; "they will convert us." Science is his religion.

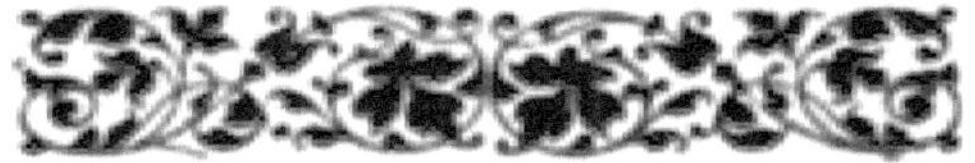

IV

"Know'st thou the house?
On columns rest its pile;
Its halls are gleaming
And its chambers smile."

—*Goethe.*

Waking early, my prayer goes up to God, with my whole consciousness borne intact. So when we miss a link in our self-calculated program of events, we look to Him, the holder of the links of us—his marionettes below.

Charley rushes in with a bundle. I speak: "Are you up, dear, and not sorry that we came?" "Haven't time. Get up and see your new dress." I sit up. "Invisible garments," he explains. I hurry to him to find only the usual feathered robes, that in tint and style give all an appearance of the feathered tribe. Tufted cap and sweeping train; wing sleeves, with which, could we fly, we would be the angels we are called.

"But where is the invisible?" I inquire.

"Dressed like everybody else, not visible, because not conspicuous," settles that problem.

I take the hint and hastily get into the suit assigned me, but not as quick as he, for he is dressed, and out, and down the hall, while I admire myself in the glittering ice-mirror walls, vanity for a moment overcoming homesickness to forget that such an unhuman-like attire, though beautiful in heaven's songsters, is more beautiful, even, in a civilized American.

In bounds Saucy—that is what we nickname Mae. "Where is my dress?"

"Here." She is soon in it, her flowing hair making her a canary. Bowing to me in mockery, she says:

"We belong here now. Where is Charley," looking around.

"Gone out," I reply.

"I am going to catch him."

"So am I."

She calls him Charley, because I do, and that he is not her uncle; nor am I her aunt, which she uses in lieu of Anna. Running out so hastily we run smack into the arms of Show Off, which we immediately see is not him, but probably his father, from the likeness, who grasps us in each hand, holding us out for inspection, saying, "I have caught two little birds that have flown to me." (Like pigeons, I wish we could fly home again.) "We have no cage here, only freedom; so now I let you go," suiting the action to the word. Cordial as sedate, I watch him as he walks down the hall and disappears. In trying to find Charley, we find ourselves in the city street.

"Mae, dear, to-day is Sunday; let us find a church," as we inspect the various houses. We select a large domed enclosure as a temple to God. Stepping to its crystal doors it opens itself to us. Within is a rest scene. Standing or sitting, all look serene, as sacred dreamy notes of melody fill the air, flower perfumed. A soothing sense of peace takes possession of us. Instead of high altar, Hebraic, or idol, or Hindoo custom, a lady and gentlemen are passing among the people, speaking kind admonitions, solemn adoration, or cheering responses. I reflect; this may be their manner of service.

The lady passing us, (who I see is our hostess) chucks us under the chin playfully, saying, "Sweets, have you come to court?"

"Court? I thought it was a church," I explain.

"What is a church?" she asks.

"Where we pray to God."

"Oh, we should do that everywhere. The earth is His court. This is only an Arc court," as she passes on. I still think it a church.

"Auntie, some are dancing; do you see?" I did. She tried the step in childish glee.

Is it a church dance? A worship mode suitable to the Arctic locality. How the Unitarians and Catholics would enjoy it. But I—my M. E. founder, Asbury, was lame, so could not dance, therefore we preach it down. Saucy, as Episcopal, sees no harm.

But now she pulls me out and waltzes me around. (I had learned the art before I joined the M. E.'s.) The glow of circulation raises my spirit to a desire to shout. I do so in M. E. denominational style, solacing my conscience thus far. Soon it pricks again.

When tired and resting I study out the scripture of this new service. Would Jesus (if here) adapt a sermon to its beneficial principles, as He had done to baptism (bath) of the crowds drawn to the river side for that purpose, obligatory in their sweltering climate? Are not all church rites illustrative of adaptations of the one worship—Spirit and Truth?

These thoughts adding so much of scriptural interpretation of new modes, adding, therefore, new program to my former stereotyped observances, I become at first slightly confused, but reserve my settled decision, until I have farther and more deeply weighed the subject. Until then, I wonder.

"What is best for us to do in such a church as this?"

I turn as I speak aloud, to see Charley by my side, who has overheard all, and coaches me. "Do? Make the earth a church, as do these people." The noon hour arrived. Refreshments of light and solid food are passed to all.

Not having got over the impression of its being a church, Mae, who has not heard the explanation, turns and says:

"Auntie, it is a sacrament! The little gum paste cups hold drink. I do not think it will harm me."

A sacrament! Would that all the churches would give each Sunday as substantial a one to Jesus' sheep and lambs, which are the poor, who go poorly fed all the week.

Seeing how strangely people sit down, by some contrivance or stiffness in their back drapery, I try my own, and being successful, am become quite at ease, as I eat, prayerfully, until satisfied. Then looking around at the beaming, social faces, I suddenly take a distrust and grasp Mae's hand: "Child, this is a saloon!" in great trepidation.

"No, auntie," she replies firmly. "No one is drunk or disorderly. It may be a hotel."

Show Off pulls my sleeve. I turn to him in benignant, grave demeanor, causing him to step back in wonder and gracious deference.

"We are Americans, I want you to know. Have you a President?"

He looks wistfully at us, to brighten soon and ask: "Do you mean your God? My mother is goddess this year. Aunt Robet takes her place when she is away visiting."

I study out the whole problem. This wayside sitting-room is a courthouse, a saloon—the latter purified—and a church in one. I am quite converted and wish ours at home would become the same, but Charley, who is still by my side, impatiently waiting to get my full attention, remarks, jokingly: "Little folks should keep out of the parlors!"

"Parlor? How do you know this is the parlor? I am sure I walked some distance to get here," I reply evasively.

"But this palace occupies some distance; you will have to look farther for a church, if there is one at all. Wait until you are better acquainted, but to-night we will attend the masque," meditatively.

"Masque? What can you imagine to be that home dissipation in this cold and pure, and pure as cold city; certainly less advanced, I hope, less perverted section of the earth. But that it is Sunday I would accompany you to investigate for missionary purposes," I reply devoutly.

"Well, it will last a week; there is no hurry," as he leaves me free to muse. So utterly definite in dissimilarity are all things here—arts, amusements, devotions, etc. I do not expect to encounter social dangers in similar guise, but must guard as conscientiously from evil under new guise. Show Off, our attending friend, does make so remarkable blunders in his attempt to apply our cultured phrases, I quite despair to get out of him by question what I wish to know. I reflect deeply, what can their church be? Can it be in happy unison, as is this human social church—to wit, parlor?

Presently I recollect that here is but one city, one people. Allowing one church to be feasible, what about different races, who have different forms of devotion that to them take the place of religion or its comparative manifestation, though religion itself is solely an act of the heart.

I imagine present before me this heterogeneous crowd. A Catholic crosses himself, a Shaker shakes, a dervish howls; Buddhists, Mahometans, and Confucians appear. Closing my eyes I wonder, could they not, one and all, do their several forms in the same building? The same "free for all" church in the same "free for all" country. Trading and walking together with mutual respect, why not worship also?

I look around and see Charley coming back. He stops short at my expression. "What are you now conjuring up?" he asks. I told, "a church, where all kinds of people worship in one building."

"Very good; when we go back home we will get one up; call it a church fair, or carnival of churches. Each and all sects to have a booth of their own. The Hindoos would put up an ox as a symbol. The Mahometans—what? a goat. The Jews a sheep. The Christians a lamb. The Chinese a roast pig. Egyptians a cat. Other pagans, somewhere—a snake. Taken altogether, an animal fair, and as all have good points, even a snake, Americans would accept all, and could, by protecting each, make them a happy family. As a cat and dog of one family live in peace under one roof, and the church symbolic animals in one farmyard, so could the principals they symbolize aid in its several good, in one church building."

I look prayerfully to him and say, regretfully, "But you don't believe Jesus is coming back."

"Yes, I do," he replies. "*Then* is He coming. For this is He waiting. Peace on earth, among the churches. Upon the cross His arms were spread. To reach around the earth, to join all churches in peace, which is brotherhood; children of God—Father."

"What would the Jew say to that?"

"They started it before Jesus. The Jewish High Priest Hillel composed the prayer, 'Our Father.'"

"Yes; but he meant it only for the Jews."

"Well! he can still be a Jew, in the new world church," and walked briskly around.

I muse. Where would be my father's place, as he is an infidel, in this many-sected or membered church. Would Jesus enfold him as a neighbor of kind heart? I think so. Entirely rejoicing in this selection of God's following, I charmingly ask Show Off, who now appears, "How long do these churches hold open?"

"Always, with Gods as relief."

"You mean ministers—but does nobody work?"

"Yes; at the schools until noon."

What! half of time for God, instead of seventh? Can the millennium have come here? Has, most likely, no one told them of the Sabbath? One day of seven? Well, we can keep both—certainly our Sabbath, and explain to these people why we do.

"One question more. Have you jails in this city? What do you do to people vicious in hot anger!"

He turns partly to me to see what I am asking; then, understanding me, he answers gravely: "Freeze them."

Aunt Robet, now off duty, takes charge of us, conducting us to her sitting-room.

But two days pass, in which we endeavor to learn the Arc language, as none except the three already mentioned can converse with us, when Charley brings forth the masque.

"Oh, yes; but it cannot be a ball nor a domino party. I am curious at your idea. If it is beneficial and delightful as what I have already seen, I will be pleased to participate," I reply, cautiously to my gentle mate, who, devoted to social assembly, and believing ennobling dancing as consistent as ennobling singing, he has no patience with my doubts.

"What am I to do?" I ask in prayer. Silent a gentle whisper breathes in answer, "It is one of the ten talents! beware of letting it rust!" One of talents, loaned us of God, and not a sin of the world? Or are the sins of the world perverted use of honorable talents, to be redeemed by us by honorable use? its omission, of condemnation.

Can I burnish and enlarge my consecration to Thee, oh God, in gay circle? Dost Thou truly love, also, happy faces? At the hall we don our costumes and are shown into a green bower, so banked with trees, shrubs, and plants there seems no space for guests. These, I soon discover, encostume everywhere about; I discover, also, much relieved, that the object is educational, only—to put us in touch with "the least of these" that God noteth.

A huge butterfly lights in front of me, greeting me cordially. So like a host I feel quite at home as a concourse of bugs, bees, and insects arise around, with waving wings, until I think I never saw before so moving a sight. A bee hummed in my ear—a sound like Charley; a mosquito sung in glee—a note like Saucy; a wasp with saucy eyes—Show Off. Moths in the windows, locusts in shady nooks, and a cricket adds its refrain. Sitting upon a scarlet ottoman, it moves off on its four feet—a live cochineal. Standing under an umbrella tree I was "darned" by a "needle" to a branch; a hopper hopped to a sheaf of wheat; lady-bugs minced; graybeards stalked around; a black-coated beetle handed me (as a weevil) a rose conserve, saying: "A 'flour' for you." I accepted it, making room for him by my side. But soon the hostess, bringing to me a "bigbug," who asked a promenade. Replying to him "May bee," the beetle gets up and snaps spitefully away.

I could see no harm, as the hours passed swiftly, teaching us a social sympathy, with this (insect) realm of the Creator, who now, as I apply my mind (talent?) to them, have always, as us, displayed love to their kind, dislike of pain, and gratefulness to benefactors. The younger danced in buoyant evidence of youthful being, the elder in touch with their delight. I saw no harm, and wished that all dancing in America could be so eminently cultivating in bodily exercise and polite demeanor.

The rooms are not close. We did not stay late to become weary.

Returning, I discover I have acquired a home interest. I see an enclosed balcony greenhouse, that line the fronts of the buildings, filled with ferns and foliage, new to me, that the sun is marvelously unfolding. They seem to grow up from the ground that must be far beneath the snow, and clinging to the ice-block wall, do not wither, for an enamel surface on the walls prevents. I then perceive why the late deep snow has spared them, snow that has been let below in covered trenches. Charley is going to pompously interview me.

"You are not so dreadfully horrified, I see. There are, you see, different grades of parties. At this you were intellectually amused and society edified. I wonder this people do not drink. I must teach them the thickening of wine blood," slightly wavering.

"Thickening of wine-tongue and brain; how did any human being ever adopt it? I earnestly believe it was water and not wine that Jesus recommended. (That has been mistakenly translated.) That being plain God's design." I speak prophetically.

"Dear," he says, "you are right; I will let the people here be temperate; thus, I believe, more enjoyable." Then coming close to me he says: "I was at the party to protect you in safety of ease, you know, so give me that due for your unrestrained mirth."

He is so autocratic in his manly assertions I become slightly overawed, when Show Off, who has had no lesson of him to regard his dignity, comes up and snaps his ear playfully. The fire darts from his eye, but I quickly make peace, using his own words: "You see, it is all right; do not be odd."

Thus quickly, everywhere, wrath arises innocently, to burn often in high flame—to indite some deed of evil intent.

Seeing Charley still cross, I converse with Show Off—ask him where my father is, that I have missed these three days. "Has he found your father's room? and is he quite happy?"

"Quite. You will never get him again," meaning that I am substituted.

This talk, though rather un-English in phrase, is so intentionally jolly, I become quite familiar, so ask: "Dear Show Off, why did the sweet Aunt Robet never get married?"

"She is going to be, when her lover comes down out of the sky."

This mysterious news sets Charley off into a roar of laughter, so I proceed: "What does he do in the sky? ride about on a star?"

"Yes; and fishes below with a line for pastime."

I look warily each side of me. "When is he coming down?"

"When the signs are right. We expected him at the Outing; since then we are unhappy."

In this lovable manner does he couple himself with his relative's heart, who now approaches, and his snap is repeated upon her glowing cheek. But she, as Charley, gets cross, and he comes back to me. I suddenly miss Saucy, to see her flaxen hair dangling out of his sleeve, and know that it is she, in childish fashion, who had done the snapping to our disconcertment.

Laughing at the innocent cause of war I turn aside to enter the court, which we are passing. Saucy seeing, drops out of her nest and hugs close to my side; the rest proceed in peace.

"Ain't it nice, Auntie, to have a church to step into all the week. You feel so safe to stop in such a place. No one expects us to buy something, or read something, or talk something. I wonder if they take up a collection. If not, the tax supports it."

"I do not believe they know what money is, though certainly they do its equivalent—work. We must find the shops and select some work ourselves."

Then, as Saucy mutters to herself, "What a queer people; no fire, no dishes, no money, no Sunday, no schools," I look around at the delightfully intelligent, as delightfully happy countenances; though the majority are lying comfortably back in their drapery supports and fast asleep. This seems to be the rest hour, and I, as Saucy lays her head in my lap, also to go to dreamland. In vision a mighty angel descends from God, down through the open dome and takes us by our wing tips, to carry us off. Hoping it is to America, I keep my eyes closed in expectation, until an unusual jar involuntarily opens them, showing the angel to be Show Off, who has deposited us safely at home on a cushion by the side of Robet.

Half uncertain, as half awake, I hum to myself the tune of "Home, Sweet Home," when Robet gets down by me and swelling her throat, warbles forth, like a bird of paradise, an entrancing melody, soothing me again to slumbers.

I awake in high fever; at least so I am told, weeks after, when I sit raised on a cushion and am able to talk. "Yes, Auntie," says Mae, "when you were in delirium you talked such strange talk. You raised up once and asked us 'What is in heaven?' I humored you and said, 'Golden streets,' but you shook your head wildly and waved your hand, saying, 'No, no; golden ice, the sun shines all night to make it."

While all regard me, lovingly, a golden point of light enters the room, *dropping at my feet*, causing consternation in the rest. Show Off hurries out and brings a tablet; reading it they point excitedly to me; the sunburst growing, they gaze in stupor.

Not until it lessens and departs do they regain composure, when I ask, "What is it?" Robet answering, "A prophecy. This sign that has never been just this way before, heralds a new era in Arc; a new people, a new land. The latter a necessity, as Arc is just evenly full."

My overbalanced visionary tendency becomes imbued with a new power. I rise in the air, spiritually, out of the open dome. Ascend to the high-poised golden points, still glowing, (my soul having left material enclosure) in the center, and look down a cavity miles wide in extent, whence drops the last golden ray; a black cloud receives it. A glint of silver lining and all is opaque.

I open my eyes to see Savant added to the circle, he was called, may be, at my faint. But what is strange, he seems to know where I had spiritually gone, and more, is expecting some revelation from me. I only slowly shake my head, when he abruptly turns away.

My new spiritual power says of him, "He is the greatest of living men." I note where he disappears to sometime search him out.

The new telepathic condition I had suddenly gone into does not entirely leave me. But takes a new form, that of outwardly statue or marble state.

Seeming cold and rigid to others, I see intuitively into their minds, read their thoughts and wishes. I am conscious at times of miraculous ability, as though I could put forth my hand, and command omniscient like.

As Robet tenderly teaches us Arc ways and diversions, I see the adaptation in foreknowledge, and surprise her and the rest, so that they are getting an awe of me, and are carefully respectful of my person.

V

"In the depths"

Mae goes out everywhere, often alone, finding the new ways and amusements of the city.

When she finds one she thinks I will enjoy, she hurries home all out of breath to take me or tell me.

She has been hunting around the halls to-day, as if there were hidden mysteries close by. I do believe she has found one. Her hair flying and eyes dancing, I go to meet her, to see what it is; getting some emotion in my own frame. "Come in here, Auntie." In there I go, like a lamb.

It is a glass entry of some sort. (I will stop to explain what I call glass, as it is not exactly, but some transparency quite serving the purpose.) Mae pulls certain knobs and lets in what— —water!

"Auntie, this is bathday. We have on bath rigs. Put on this helmet with its tubes above for breathing."

I do so, as the water deepens. She opens a gate now, and a flood rushes in, and takes us off our feet, which we regain by use of our elastic breathing tubes.

We pass through the gate to all the glories of the sea. A sea bath—sea mosses under our feet, shells piled in heaps, fern trees waving.

Mae dashes out and hides from view. I discover her, but cannot hold her with my wet hands.

We hear a song. In the door of a crystal grotto stands a mermaid. "Come into my bower, and I will give you amber. I am a sister of seven who combs her long hair in the deep."

Ascending steps of dainty harpshell, we tread an anemone carpet where is a crowd of people.

Games are in order on rock ruby stands, in which I become engrossed, as a "sister" plays a cameo-mandolin; another singing a rollicking song of the sea, ending in sobs, for those who come down in ships.

There is sea-dancing—liquid symphony. I see Charley in his native element, precluding tears or weeping for joy.

We round out on a tower top, and board a nautilus with unfurled sail. We ride over a gold fish "gilt-edged" school, and a bank of red sea berries that holly-like call up to us "Merry Christmas."

Furling our sail, we drop down into the entry, which we empty, and strange, our garments are dry.

We emerge among our friends. A sweep of robes is so close passing me, I look up at the colossal face. It is Robet, but a strained, nervous look forbids me to follow.

Toppling upon the hem of her robe, I am carried perforce in her company. She stops in a conservatory, where one grand tree is growing, and bends down a branch. I look to see it and all the tree transcribed with names—a veritable family tree. More distraught, she speaks in a loud-pitched voice, down into the face of Charley, who has followed me (seeing him not), "Have you a pedigree?" He colors up in wrath, then takes a tablet from my chatelaine, and places it in her hand, which awakes her. Smiling, she says, "I did not mean you." Charley reacting from anger to hilarity, seizes a twig, crying. "I will write a pedigree," as a red pollen drops, touching up my cheeks. "They need it," he says, and goes for Mae, who now comes, and soon she glows like an Indian.

When he is gone, Mae, in order for ablution, opens near by a door, that is outwardly a picture. (More mystery).

Can it be the secret sanctum of Savant, that I have so vainly hunted? Father sits in an easy chair deeply engaged with a pictured script. I look around but see no books or apparatus—a cheerful, cosy room only. I look over father's shoulder as he turns the papyrus leaf, holding over it a microscope. I catch sight of the meaning. Giving a sudden cry, he arouses to my presence. He takes me on his knee, and we follow together the tiny pictured lines of a story.

Anon a kitten purrs by me; I look up and see the host intently reading my expression in his own absorbed, telepathic style. Genially smiling, he takes my two hands, and kneeling places them on his head, thus confessing his service to my will. Though in my new normal state, I feel to deprecate myself, and smile in humblest mode, as he rises and sits next us in similar seat.

Before we turn to our occupation, an incandescent glow falls upon the page, causing us to raise our eyes quite wonderingly. The light emanates quite mysteriously from Robet, whom I had not before observed as thus illumined. I see in her hand a lighted lantern, which she is studying, or the shining words upon it.

That these latter are possibly a code of rules is determined by her action. Sinking down at Savant's feet, she asks, "Do give me some new plan for court to-day."

"I will give you one," speaks up father. She turns full to him.

"It is lawyer, a word signifying welfare."

I was aware my English language was prolific of varied meanings. I am pleased to hear this development. "Law," he continues, "transposed is 'well;' yer is 'fare.'"

Miss Robet has caught his idea, and elaborates it. "When I go into court, the good word shall be welfare; when I come out—farewell," and is gone.

Dear Robet, what is her secret sorrow, that she hides in her tender breast? Her genial soul should have no rebuff. Why is her intended away, as I have heard?

Quite changeable in mood, as is Show Off, her great chum, who gets it from his mother, the latter a triplet sister with Robet, and now on a visit to the other triplet sister.

We now give attention to the story before us, but so loudly sounds a refrain in my ears, "Savant before you is the greatest of living men," until I become impatient, and ask, "how great?" "Ask him hidden knowledge," refrains back to me.

What can it mean?

I will treat him to some unsettled points in spiritual doctrine to test his lore.

VI

Immortality of the soul is an universal instinct.

Phil. Schaff, D. D.

Looking to where he sits, I study one in my mind, and observe father sees my abstraction. I can tell by a wrinkling around his eyes, he is preparing himself for enjoyment of the debate.

"What is the breath of life?" I at last ask ingenuously.

"Oh, I can answer that. I have found it out since I have been here. That is an easy question. It is, my dear, electricity, which we assimilate into spirit. Simple in explanation. The electric soul batteries of our organism thus supplied by God, the maker of souls, drawn in with our breath." Quite suavely preaches my father to me.

"Yes, but there are two electricities; how could we take both and live?"

"There are two electricities, assuredly. They assimilate; the assimilation is life."

I feel dubious, but see clearer as he proceeds.

"The earth has negative electricity, the other positive, or masculine, comes from the sun, uniting to life."

Suddenly I burst out, "That makes the sun our father. Pray, who is God, who made the sun?" The eye wrinkle deepens. "In that case, our grandfather."

I scorn to smile.

"Does this soul life have bodily sense after death?" I again venture a second question.

"Yes, and bodily sustenance in the air, where is body material, tho' invisible."

I clasp my hands to my head, and rush out of the room. But close behind me is Savant, who is pleased to wish more acquaintance.

I overcome my awe, but do not care to inquire on abstruse subjects. We go out into the street, and traverse its length before I am attracted by a special diversion. Entering a hall to rest, we are witness, to me, of an utterly, and at first inconceivable, exhibit, unheard of before novelty. It is the paradoxic act of a Concert, or Opera, without sound—seen and not heard. Upon the stage are rows of lights (reflections) graded in size like the string of a harp. Raising and lowering these in varying figure by skilful players constituted the performance. The changing (not unison) melodies in grave or gay parts, or intermingling, swaying my emotions. I lean back in rapture.

I am studied by my escort, who has been addicted thus, since first he looked at me.

The green sward beneath our feet, as on all floors, prevents the unpleasant custom of stamping. Soon the walls moved in and out, portraying drama. A row of graded boys and girls also, carrying dolls in wickers that they stood up against the walls, bowed their heads and waved their hands in pantomime melody. Marching away, the boys carried the dolls.

We were quite diverted, laughed heartily, stamping on the sward floor, that produced no sound.

"We will tell Mae about this," I remarked. "Let's go home and send her here."

We hurried to the palace to find her under a divan with her head out, though covered by the flowing robe of a doll (mother bunch) into which her hands had been made. Charley has to keep the people away, who are greatly mystified as interested, while he is asking questions, answered by bowing or head shaking of the sorceress.

Suddenly he answers for the doll in ventriloquism, from which they back in amazement.

When it is over and Mae released, so great is their awe of us, I seek to enhance it. I take my watch and convince them it is alive.

This quite overcomes them. I turn to see Charley, slowly at first, then swifter nod his head up and down, as tho' some unusual resolve was engrossing his calculations, soon I find out. Coming around to me, he says: "I feel a call in my soul to initiate this people to serve our God. I will take this almighty dollar," suiting in action, he goes through some wizard tricks.

We are tired before they. "Do tell us some more," they ask.

The next day they are still curious, and keep us engaged in exhibit.

We advert to our railroads, telephones, etc., to their confusion, as we have no samples. Catching in their perplexity some similarity to their own achievements, they bring forward and strive to teach us how they move articles by a *solution*. Chairs and street cars in their wizard propulsion are solved.

"Is it a vegetable or mineral?"

"It is animal."

Their explanation as greatly confounded us.

"We get it from a fish, which Savant found when he was last over the ice. He saw the ice strangely cracking to find the queer fish. Grasping it, there was an explosion of sound. He brought some home, but they are hard to raise." Finding us continue in solicitude to understand, they treat us in exchange of our revelations. Our story reminds them of one to match it.

One day explaining to Robet how Unit ladies make themselves young-looking by cosmetics and pencils, she says briskly, "I will take you to-morrow where they make themselves old and wise-looking. You will be pleased; it is a fine city."

After dinner we go. Arriving, I see the houses are crackled in straight or curved lines of beautiful design. Lines are the fashion.

The costume was striped in pattern. The sward carpet was stems in graceful arrangement.

The table for light refreshments was a single piece, curving in rings from top-vase to cake and lower fruit-trays down to numberless seals, all curls of its octopus dimensions.

As Robet said, the special fad in face garniture of the ladies, as well as the gents, was aged penciling in lines. The marks of wisdom sit quaintly on young brows. Drooping mouths are traced to upward curve. Sad eyes smile; laughing are deepened in thought.

The ribbon-dressed babies are ribboned into similar hammocks, to be swung back and forth.

Their mode of worship at court was to stand in straight lines, like soldiers of God.

Their games are sticks (kindergarten) which they also work into ingenious devises of cabinets and stands. The arches of apartments decorated thus.

Their adieu was straightening of the fingers.

When on our way home, I kiss Robet. My statue sense is wearing away. Still yet, I seem to see the past and future. Interior of minds. An aura-cathode light clarifies. I ask; to answer; my own questions.

"Are spirits before birth individuals?"

"No, only in bulk, combining chemically at birth."

"Dangers in this life, are there dangers in the next?"

"There are." I listen to myself statue like.

At last I ask Savant, "What is it?" He is puzzled as I, and questions me on my church faith. I tell him about Adam and Jesus; the latter to tell us all mysteries, when he comes in the clouds. He is intensely interested. I get my bible and read to him day after day.

Much affected one day, he looks up to ask: "May not he the God have sent this upon you to make you his second forerunner?"

Is the secret solved? Am I the herald-searchlight to His path?

(And is he—the Savant—my mission aid)? Near by me, concealed by art-screen, I hear a sob, and see a yellow gleam of hair drop on a loving shoulder. Saucy sobs up to a face, thinking deeply. "Cholly," coaxing, "what shall we do—will she go up into the sky?"

A jerk of the shoulder straightens up the head, and sobers the grotesque grief of its face. "No, you do not know her. She is smart, I allow, but not so smart as she thinks." (I feel so funny as I listen). "She is weak yet from her illness is all."

"O!" ejaculates Saucy as she relapses to her usual self.

Something rustles under my feet. I pick up a piece of American newspaper. Saucy says behind me, "That was around my lunch mamma put up. She is still looking, I suppose," deeply sighing.

I carefully read each precious word. A short but torn excerpt on science contains this: "I said one good thing of the soul. That it was electrified after death."

I am at sea. It was not Savant's lore, but my father's, who had deceived me. I go to him with the scrap. He reads and smiles, then takes up a leaf near him. Holding over it a microscope, I see on it a picture of cloud lightening taking a spirit to the sky. A wielder of that lightening concealed afar off. I am at sea again.

I take to studying the leaves myself, seeing how useless to question Savant.

Charley and Mae too study with me. Still, the latter jealously watches Savant. Whose modes and agencies are new. Though I see magnetism appear at times, I cannot tell how produced (he works in an alcove one side).

Every morning I am a fixture here, studying, marking a place on the register to visit in the afternoon. So safe am I, now a citizen, I often go alone. Charmed as "Van Winkle," stay long away.

I am surprised they show no solicitude. Mae one time is absent a week. Alarmed I go to Savant. He takes the register telephones of her position. Then in a shining leaf shows me in picture what has passed to her. I feel to get up and hug him. But hug Charley who is come. "You had better go after her," he says. "Why, I know all she does." "Yes, but you should direct what she does," wisely.

I look to the leaf. A new impress is coming. Behind her as she is backing unconsciously toward it, is an open crevasse trench in use by a workman. I startle the air with a scream to Savant, "Call me," says Charley, authoritatively, who looks on the plate, to call Savant himself. The latter seeing the dilemma, without leaving his laboratory, touches a button, that closes the crevasse behind Mae, as she steps on it safely. I hug Charley convulsively.

VII

"Logic is logic. That's what *I* say."

—O. W. H.

My husband, always so loving, so bonny and practical, has become sober and long-faced, no shadow of a smile. No hop, skip and jump, like Saucy Mae. Even she he passes absent-minded. If she pulls his sleeve, he does not heed, so she follows him around to find what the matter is. As she makes a body-guard, I leave her to watch him.

He has just come out of Savant's room, absorbed in some papers, he carefully carries in his hand, assorting them as he noiselessly walks along, the genius behind failing to get a peep at their contents. Hearing me approach, he hastens to conceal them in the shrubbery, disappearing himself.

Saucy having lost him, takes up with me, and we run out and up the street, looking in at various places. Seeing familiar faces in a crowd at an opera house, we join them.

Seeing us, the crowd gives way, and gets up in front, where we become the cynosure of the audience (the performance not having commenced), who look from us to the stage, as if in connection, enigmatical to us.

Puzzled no longer, we see Charley come out and take position as speaker.

Our mouths as well as eyes open in wonder. What will happen next?

With preoccupied bearing, he explains our discovery of iron, that raised man from savagery to civilization, builds ships and houses. It was well we were before him and appreciated his discourse (the home reminiscence starts the old pain) for the audience do not understand a word he says, but connecting his gestures, they oddly imitate the latter.

He turns to us and changes to an abstruse subject, not at all congenial to him.

"Americans concede three natures to man and five senses. I will show him to possess seven natures, each represented by a sense." We are quite attentive. "Touch, first, by his palm, denoting his acquiring nature." I clap my hands. "Taste, second, by his tongue, denoting his sustenance nature." I muse to myself, do we kiss because we are cannibals, and would like to eat the one we kiss?

"Social, third, by his lips, denoting his impress nature." O yes, that is why we kiss. "Vibrative, fourth, his ear, denoting his emotional nature." I think him quite a phrenologist. Mae is some dazed. "Atmospheric, fifth, by his nose, denoting his steam nature." Mae sends up a prolonged shout.

"Solar, sixth, by his eyes, denoting his mental nature." I shake my finger at him.

"Soul, by his hair, denoting electric spirit nature." I come to my feet, raising both hands, as he proceeds.

"The hair as covering or ornament of the head has not received sufficient dignity. As telegraph lines of divine construction communes with God, raises its value." I place my hands on each of his shoulders, as he finishes impressively.

"Above the mind, summit of senses, its own power only has revealed it even to sight."

Remembering him coming out of Savant's studio, I am not surprised.

But I continue the thread. Does this theory contravene the immortality of the soul, teach dissolution with the body? O, no.

The operator back of the telegraph machine does not integrate with the machine. The telegraph wires down do not signify the operator to be in the same condition.

VIII

My spirit lies, with dreamful eyes,
Beneath the walls of Paradise.

I catch sight of Show Off coming leisurely toward us. Has he caught the last part of the lecture, and is he, too, of a studious disposition. For raising his eyes intelligently, he continues the discourse. "Still we are made of dust!" (What can *he* know of dust?) "Birds," going on, "are made of trees, for their feathers are little branches. Fishes are of waterbirth—their scales little drops. Beasts of grass, with coats of grass fur. Sheep of snow wool." I am wool gathering. "Reptiles have clod skins. We are only of the dust—marble, granite or otherwise." I decide to read him Genesis some day.

But now he speaks up more blithe. "We are going to-morrow to Aunt Roban's house, where my mother Roba is, to get her," winking his eye at Saucy.

We are delighted as we return, all together. I look at the streets and people, not knowing I shall see them no more forever.

The next morning, that is getting very late, we are placed in an open sleigh, to try the new snow, in making the trip. As it is a gala day, called Inning Day, so everybody is out. "Will everybody be at Roban's?" I ask Show Off, who is holding Saucy by my side.

"Yes, and more too, for the Traveler will be there," he replies moodily.

"Who is he, and where does he travel?"

"Up in the sky on his air star."

"And what does he do up there?" I smile.

"He fishes below with a line."

I look warily each side or me.

"Do you like him?"

"Yes, but he wants me to marry his daughter."

"Well?"

"She won't have me, as she loves my cousin, Aunt Roban's son. Her father expects our betrothal at this time." He stops a moment, then resumes. "He is engaged, himself, to be married to Aunt Robet, who does not dare to tell him of his coming disappointment."

"How did she, so gentle, ever fancy so douty a man?"

"It was at a ride. The cavalry were going by so swift she became dizzy and was falling, when he by a deft move put her back. When he appears, ever since, she is like affected. He is coming now."

With a start, I look up to the sky, which is clear. Then I look about at the celebrators, thinking he may be come to earth, and be among them. And though I see a strange mist in the distance, I become occupied in studying the various modes of conveyance close around. Of every odd design, one vehicle is oddest. It is a round glass globe that rolls over and over, bearing its inmates upright, ballasted in the interior. It has only ladies, so I look ahead.

Ahead is a bridge, shaped like a flight of stairs (rests for the horses). Around the farther tower arches—strong supports of the suspended ends—a mist is twining and winding, glistening peculiarly. Show Off seeing my intent gaze looks there, and hastily takes from his father's pocket a glass and absorbedly scans the mist. I had forgotten the Traveler's approach, of shock to Robet, who leans back her head gasping faintly. But directly over us is the shocking man, on a high seat, over high runners, between which glides our humble sleigh. At Show Off's shout, he looks down, his stern face relaxing genially, recovering Robet.

Thus disturbed, Show Off drops the glass, which I pick up, wonderingly.

One look, and I am curious too. For deep within the luminous vapor are human beings, lace seated and draped. They are singing, their countenances reflecting the inspiring symphony. Studying closely, I detect a peculiarity of expression, as if masculine and feminine are combined, both strong and tender. Coming swiftly, and bending low, they must brush us as they pass. A child in front of adult, eyes exhilarantly my exotic bouquet. I select a dainty bud, and raise it over my head. The gust shuts my eyes. But I feel a tiny touch that wisps away my bud. From our slow journeying, we are too late to make our address at Roban's, before the election, which occurs to-day. So proceed to that function. Seated comfortably upon the Central Plaza, a nice esplanade covered with rugs, we are scarcely seated when two ladies and a gent approach us, who by their family resemblance are no doubt sisters of Robet. One hugs her tremblingly. The other is hugged vigorously by Savant, his wife Roba. She is, though of exact likeness, still of different temperament from the others. More sedate, quite stately, though none the less lovable. When Savant puts my father with his silver hair and shining black eyes on her lap, she is quite awe struck. When my father reaches up and kisses her reverently on the cheek; she is more nonplussed still, and takes her muff to sit him on.

The gent is no doubt the husband of the other sister, who snaps his fingers at Charley, when he wishes he did not, for the latter bites it viciously; then rubbing the bite over, he lays his cheek on it, in penitence. He is forgiven, but not taken up on his lap, but I am instead, and smile profusely to keep the peace. Saucy is on Roban's shoulder, and chatting like a parrot into her ear, which just suits this lady, she answering as glibly.

"O, how late you are! We could not wait for you, but left the castle open and came on. Has the Traveler come?" That individual passes without seeing us. Before we hail him, we hear music of a band approach. The melody is whistling as will Boreas shortly whistle over the land.

Conducting two lines in grand march, in election mode, headed by the chosen Mayor and Mayoress, respectively, or as they call them, god and goddess.

The evolutions ended, the two lines join, and the crowd standing, all sing:

> E'er the sun our father leaves us
> He, as a parent, leads us
> To the indoor mother's side
> To spend the winter tide.

The candidates, now in full view, are recognized by Robet with consternation. "Roban's son, and his daughter," are her startling words.

We all turn silently toward Roban's home. The ceremonies now ended. The new city officers, receiving congratulations around, also join our party, staying in our rear.

The castle supposed to be open is not so now, but is double barred inside against us, as we arrive.

Through the crystal portal, we see in the center court, sitting nonchalantly as revengefully, the man who rode over us. We are out in the cold, and what is worse, quite hungry.

Savant calls out, "Hello, neighbor." He arises and is about to come forward, when his daughter laughs out, "Now papa, good papa," which stops him, and he turns square his back to us.

Beyond and near to him is a revolving plant stand, reaching high above his head. A plant is moving mysteriously. I see my father under a leaf (I had not missed him). He is arranging something under a blossom. I cannot tell what.

Now before us and at our feet down drops the nervous Robet, who cannot keep her dignity longer.

Around goes the plant stand and sounds out this word, which is from a phonograph (placed by father) in Arc, "Look ye." Around again, it is above him. "Looky," now one side, now behind. Mystified, the stolid man looks around as directed, not at our faces, where he will see the mirthful countenance of his daughter, but at our feet where he sees a countenance pale and in tears. The spell is broken, and as father leaps on his shoulder like a good fairy, he lets us in.

A castle band now starts up to a tune resembling the snapping of a fire, reminding us of the day of the Inning Fireside. Now crackling forth with renewed zest, the people arrange themselves in cavalcade, and slowly march, with spiral inclination, around the hall, towards its center.

Robet, supported by her lover, pulls me out of her bag to amuse him, much to my ill-will. But father winks to me over his head, and pulls his hair. Nearing the center of the room, the Traveler firmly and (I see his daughter grimacing close by) turning from the pleading Robet goes out of the room, and out of the house, disappearing down the street.

Wondering at this action, I look for information, to the center gathering, I see a crystal floor in circle shape, with round divans in its center. I am mystified as we are seated on this divan, and look down at the crystal floor. I get a great start, for my feet seem to be standing up in the sky, so far down is the crevasse below, whence comes up a brilliant glow, the only light in the apartment now, as blinds and shades are placed to protect it. Whence this light arises, I cannot imagine, as the sun is not in focus, or other light.

I take a great like to Roban, who is as friendly as vivacious. I get upon her lap to hear her chat.

"Good-bye," she says, "my upper sky home, for the winter. My plant stand you may rest until spring (outing as she calls it)."

I am mystified why the people stop to sit here, as there is no table.

With a slight jar, the crystal floor now loosens, and more surprise, descends. Now beneath the floor, the light is increasing, and a warmth also, at which we cast off our wraps, displaying evening costume of home. The car, I now see it to be, is in triplet decoration. Triplet bell clusters favor us with melodies. I wonder how long we are descending, when jar, sway, float, as in water. I look about. "Where, oh where is this?"

We are on the bosom of a broad river in a scene of tropical beauty and grandeur.

Mae and Charley, as I, are as completely surprised, the others enjoying its fulness.

"Eden, Eden, garden paradise, whence came you here?" I weep beside myself in joy. Is this what explorers seek? But they will never get here. It is hemmed in by the iceberg, two-edged swords, as effectually as the other one of our first parents.

Roban asks, "What is Eden?" I told her of Adam's, and the one to come down to us from the sky. "No," she says gravely, "the city will grow up to God."

Is San Francisco (San-Zion) thus growing?

I see that Show Off, unlike all the others, is in a growing state of excitement. I jump down quickly and climb to his side, where he is leaning on the railing of the barge, looking expectantly into the water. I punch him vigorously. "Tell me, tell me, how came this river down here, and its vicinity?" He answers vaguely, not looking up, "By the melting of the under ice."

"Yes, but to be a flowing river?"

"We confined it for safely, by dykes and jetties," becoming quite distraught at some inward thought. Does he mourn the Traveler's daughter?

Roban has followed me, and now explains to me more fully.

"When the river got to going good, it melted the ice above clear through to the sky." I look up at the faraway opening.

"The sky opening," she continues, "vegetation started." I look now eagerly at the nearby banks in begonia bloom, and crowned with palms. Long aisles of verdure penetrate the vista, closed by green sheen. One specialty of form is general, that of vine-climbing and up-looking.

Returning my attention to Roban, she resumes her coaching. "Cities too sprang up. We will stop now and get some of the luscious fruit," as the car-barge slows and draws up to an orchard station.

We who have listened spellbound to explanation are getting over our paralysis, and are the first to jump on land. Saucy running crazy is soon lost to view. We dart hither and thither with delight, pulling mangoes, decking ourselves with orchids, mimicking songsters. I wonder no more where they get their conservatory plants. When a bell calls us to dinner.

In a bower, vine surrounded and bird enlivened, we draw up to board, not a board, either—none, or saws to make them are in the land, it is a great lily leaf, hardened and enameled.

Indentations serve for places. The food, on small leaf trays, arises from the table center dummy like. It is in mouthful-size pastry cups (that makes me think of home tarts), blending grain food with other kinds. Raised with the fingers, nothing can be neater.

The seats are leaves. Springs raise us smaller people to a level with the rest.

I observe greatly rejuvenated looks in us and say to Charley: "Do you see we are getting younger?" He stops picking a pomegranate. "Certainly. It is the purity of the atmosphere. Have you noticed, my dear, that there has been no dust since our arrival? And, tho' the sun is constantly shining, no one carries a shade or is overheated. Ah, this is the Country to live in!" Smacking his lips before starting in again on the fruit.

"Glorious Arc!" I can not say it enough! None other place like thee on earth in gorgeous marvels! Nearest to God above! I could climb a Pole to see Him, hadst thou one! I look around to see the climatic effect upon my aged father; but he is not here. I remember he may be yet on the Traveler's shoulder for farther travel. This somewhat modifies my charm—for a short time only, then I give way like the rest to the fulness of this Inning Reception. As bright tints float around in the air, on the water, and foliage, I wonder what pencil but God's could put them there.

As we return to the barge Saucy at my elbow grasps my sleeve, saying, "Auntie, did you see the team that draws the barge? If you did not, look this time, now."

What?—what? Crocodiles?

I stagger back, then renerve myself, reassured that what I had always supposed so hideously untamable could be well broke, kept well in hand, presenting an innocent pair of open countenances.

"How odd the water is Auntie," says Mae, when we are calmly seated. She is looking over the side, then rises and crosses to the other. "It is high up on one side and low down on the other."

Robet speaks without looking up, her eyes intent on her nephew, leaning moodily on the railing. "The river flows sideways."

"How—how can it?"

"It melts on its inward side, freezing on its outward again."

"Making ice for cool drinks," says the child.

While dropping in the incline I commenced a study of the triplet sisters. Observing them distinct in style with the river people (of whom they are, and are now to visit their parents, Robet has said), I will describe them.

Tall and sinuous from a constant looking up to the sky. A changeable coloring or iridescence enhances their supple attenuation. Robet, when musing, as I have related in the arbor above, was sober gray-eyed; when demanding so proudly Charley's pedigree, intensely black-eyed; then, in tears recovering him, her eyes were blue, vapor-covered lakes. Seeing this variableness repeated in her sisters I decided it to be constitutional; I looked to see if it was a water reflection. No, for it is not on us others.

Roban and Roba are on each side getting acquainted.

To start conversation instructive to myself I ask the gracious ladies; "How was it before the country was dyked into a river?"

"We were not born then. Our father was contractor and has told us how unpleasant were the freshets and disasters yearly."

"Whole nations were swept away. Did you not find any down there?" Roba relates.

"I never heard, though Adam, the father of all mankind, was very large in size, the people became smaller afterwards."

Looking earnestly at me I see them change slowly from blonde to a gray tint, bending their heads in reflection, (I see with great surprise.)

"We have always been large. I think it is the cold zone; its slow revolution causing it. The torrid, as Charley says, with its far revolution is very hot." A flush on her face as she raises her serpentine head.

"It gets more sun and the people there are larger, too," I correct.

Their eyes, my surprise increasing, turn brown as she steadfastly gazes.

"Then it is not the cold that makes us grow, but preserves us, giving us great age. We are millenniums old," she breathes gently, chestnut-haired.

I am transfixed. When able to look up I see a halo round her head; a slight toss and it is dislodged in a ring leaving her in violet.

Going on with her deductions a dawn color follows her words.

"Our great size is due to our daylight."

"But we have as much as you, tho' more subdivided," I correct again.

"You have not counted our winter daylight," she persists.

"Winter daylight? What is that?" I inquired.

"From the center of Arc is always arising, from a deep cavity there, a constant glow, Aurora! In summer it is not seen, but all winter we bask in its light."

"How is that? I supposed Aurora only sent up fitful lights."

"Instead, this constant, interspersed with fitful sputterings, that send the flame so high, lower zones do gaze upon it." Closing a phosphor color enfolds us, then rises above. Notes in the waves—trumpet notes, conducted toward us till they sound all about us. A mist-like spray is rising around. Looking out I am startled to see a large company of people standing on the water in the center of the river playing lily-tube trumpets as in graceful ease they dance a stately minuet.

Raising aloft their tubes they spray the air with perfumed drops, which, catching the rays of the sun through the ice-cleft, a glorious rainbow arch settles above as we draw to shore and alight upon a wharf of lily pads.

The sun passes on ahead having kept such even pace with us all day that it had appeared to be standing still in the sky. The heat had called for our light dress. To-morrow it will be in lower horizon.

We have arrived in a city that is like the people, tall and pointing high—a city of slim, needle-like towers.

Passing toward a mansion I turn to tell Show Off to pattern after the young man with the river dancers, looking so like him who was gay, when lo! he is not with us.

"It was Show Off himself, Auntie, I saw him put on the funny boat-shoes and drop overboard."

"Who is the young lady he was bending over," I inquire.

"I do not know, some more complications I expect," inimicably.

"Saucy," I say comically, "he is not for you."

"I know it," sighing, "I will never have him to carry me around on his shoulder."

What are Savant and Roba doing ahead, walking up the outside of a tower residence? Truly they are, and our turn come we see plenty of steps and walk up too.

Arrived at the second story we enter a low gate into a circular room the size of the tower. Around the outside is a row of seats which we proceed to occupy. In front of us are promenading round and round the river dancers, buoyant in youth.

From these Show Off leads a lustrous river maid and presents as betrothed to his family, who can but smile upon them, except Robet who gets quite pale. Whispering to her, "Cheer up, Auntie, love is might," he draws her to her feet and waltzes her around until she is hopeful again. We all get up and dance in honor of the betrothal.

When we sit again the others wait upon us from the center of the room, which is a mass of flowers, fruit and pastry.

The dance starting on, Robet says to me, "Let's go out."

"All right."

She touches a button and we elevate to the top of the tower. A branch of clove-scented vine brushes my cheek. Seeing me peer down Robet hands me a glass to see into the shade of the tropical park beneath.

Seeing me occupied she bends down her head in meditation. Then sighs and sighs to herself, bravely struggling with these breakers in her love stream.

I am examining each detail in the grounds beneath. From the palm leaf that is so strong Saucy runs up and slides down it. Tired of this she picks an odd blossom in shape of a tiny cupid with drawn bow. At her touch shoots the tiny arrow and to break in fragrance. Would that all Love's arrows were so sweet. I suddenly realize where the verdure of Upper Arc is produced, as familiar forms greet me, faithfully growing up as to the summer day. Where are they now? Glass protected in upper arbor.

Tired of the Cupids, Mae now rolls over and over in the grass with abandon of childish glee until she suddenly comes upon two lovers—Show Off and Serpenta (I have named) which latter smiles her a welcome, stooping down to raise her to where they sit, a long, slim, rope looking swing or hammock. But Mae starts back with a scream, which makes me look close. O, dear, it is the live folds of a boa constrictor.

I get faint as Robet looks up and takes in the situation.

"Do not fear," she says, "it does not eat children, it is better fed."

Imagining she is laughing at me I brace up to great bravery, asking, "Can I ride, too?"

"Yes, we will go down, look out;" the latter in reference to the chair upon which I sit—one of a row of seats around the lower edge, facing outward. I look quite curiously and assure myself its rails are in front as on each side of me, inclosing me quite secure. Connecting it to her own, she presses on them heavily downward. Feeling warned, as curious, I feel the top bend over forwards, still more. I hold quite fast. My head is now where my heels have been. This is not all; increasing the velocity we complete the revolution, and repeat it to the foot of the tower, where I come standing, red with vexation (the idea of a lady of my age rolling down the side of a house), my temperate zone stomach quite upset.

But "click" at the top. There is Roba in similar chair, who signifying that she will join us is about to round the edge. I recover my temper in anticipation of being witness to her acrobatic descent—stateliness combined. But no; she slowly goes over, smoothly, down to the bottom dignifiedly—right side up with care. I turn reproachfully to Robet.

"I thought you were in for a frolic," she says innocently.

This restores my gaiety and we return to the arbor with zest and join the jolly crowd who are making the garden ring. They make room for me on the boa, where I ride, the danger enhancing the delight. I regret to get down for others. As I do so, the great graceful head of the boa swings close to me, the mouth opens, the eyes dart fire; then next I discover it is an art manufacture.

"There are real ones, Auntie, but they do not let strangers ride."

A storm is brewing, as I hear a thunder peal; no clouds above—some are in the vista, rapidly drawing near, close to the ground. What an odd hurricane! No; with bounds and roars a herd of white lions rush into near precinct and wait, low crouched. Their long pink-tinted manes make them so handsome I forget they are fierce. Some are grand and nervous looking, others young and playful. Calling one of the latter by name, it wriggles from the rest to go to Show Off. Saucy stepping up too frightens it back; but trying again he coaxes it to him, where Saucy also strokes it, saying: "You must give it to me to take to America," bless her.

A shout and he strides its back, then with merry bounds, race and glee, they give us quite a circus.

My attention is called to my side by a mysterious self-satisfied lisp. I turn to see Charley who is taking notes for future lectures. I look over to get the train of ideas. What do I see—"How lions dance in our country; machines put in their mouths, they sing."

"O Charley, what a drop. I had counted on your wonderful conversion, and here are you improvising wonders."

Roban is getting social. "There are not many lions now. They were dangerous; the city filling up has thinned them out. Do you want one?"

I am still in chagrin, so answer crossly the sweet-tempered lady, "What for? Will it take me home on its back?"

She eyes me sideways, still serene. "Do you want to go home?" I choke up in golden silence. "When you want to go the Traveler will take you," complacently.

Roused to ire at my earnestness being taken for jest, I launch out disrespectfully, "That crusty man would drop me over an iceberg and think his duty done."

She does not heed me as her sister Robet is now approaching quite rosy cheeked, and is about to dance me up and down, which I never allow, when I can help myself.

Roban says to her sorrowfully, "The little dear is going home with the Traveler."

I smile, then say to Robet, "When he and you are married I will go." Then I eye her sideways.

O what a drop! My Charley untruthful! When he says my church raises money untruthfully in its fairs and suppers.

I was about to have him teach this people how Christ incarnated is to come on the earth from the clouds. Shall I now do so instead? Yes. I select the Traveler's daughter as one quite wayward, and say: "Dear lady, an American (oh no!) a man like us little folks is in the sky; some day he will come down and make us golden streets," smiling broadly.

"What is gold?" she inquires.

"Something harder than rock."

"'Twill hurt your feet; grass is better."

"Glass houses," I continue. "That is fine."

"No one will marry." O what a face she makes.

"No dear little children?" she pleads.

"No one dies," I continue.

"O how nice and old."

"Always fruit and flowers." I feel I am getting along nicely. When she asks:

"How is that? they being the children of tree and plant marriage."

"I never thought of that," but continue:

"All dead will come to life."

"Where is the room for them?"

"All bad men will be killed off."

"Who will kill them off?"

"He that comes out of the sky."

"Their spirits would haunt him."

"He would kill their spirits, too."

"None but God can do that."

"He is the Son of God."

"O, is God married?" so impiously, I lose heart. But Roban comes to my aid. With shining expectant eyes she now interrogates me.

"When will He come?" I shake my head.

"*Who* will He bring to life?" persisting.

"Those who love Him. O dear, dear Roban, do you love God?" I am pleading for a soul.

"That I do," is her positive confession.

"Do you love His Son?" my hands clasped toward her.

"Anything that belongs to Him," so beatifies me I spring to my feet to declare:

"Then *you* will be saved, for love is the fulfilling of the law."

Drops sprinkle all about. I look back of me to see Saucy with inspired face who has been listening. Thus bestowing this rite upon this new convert, who strangely takes on a serious look.

"I know whom you mean," she says. "He does like this," pointing her hands as in prayer. What can she mean?

"He comes here to teach us."

"Who, who? It cannot be He, the Son. Does the spirit of an apostle transfigured appear in this city—this city of love? I am astounded."

"He says that in a century hence electricity will create a human being."

What can she mean? Is the camera-eye, telephone-ear to be supplemented by a dynamo head, put on locomotive lungs and stood on wheel feet?

Truly here is sympathy in Arc for such invention.

Twenty-four hours without sleep. I yawn so terribly. Robet anxiously straightens me out on a chair for repose.

I dream in shadow of friends and home. Saucy's mother hugs her close.

Next my chair is moved easily along and I open my eyes in an ice grotto, where a large company is assembled, whom I imagine are the many relatives.

As older people, like them in feature are occupying special chairs of state—the parents?

The change to cool arbor from summer heat is so greatly refreshing I regain animation.

At the parents' request, we are placed on pedestals for exhibition.

"Are all so small?" they inquire.

"We are medium. There are midgets and giants," we reply.

"How greatly you have multiplied. How great the size of the earth in comparison with Arc. You do more wonderful acts in proportion as you have more land to work upon."

They place their hands upon our heads in token of membership in their family.

IX

"There is magic in the air."

Another pedestal is being occupied by Show Off and Serpenta, who are dancing a betrothal. In graceful pose and gesture, his movements are an epic poem in majesty and solid grandeur, hers the duplicate shadow of his, with interlacing quicksteps. An ice dance on the ice, the feet not raised off. The complication of steps is insidious to the eye in their noiseless turns. Noiseless? rising on the air is a melody, that grows and lessens, produced by the swift slipping. Ending in smooth tone as true love ought.

When it is over, and the company dispersed, I wander around by myself to soon get lost in the tangle of halls, which labyrinth every way. Just here are niches in the walls with statues of people and animals like life. Here is a family group. The host is deep in Arc news ball (writing rolled up) his wife is crossing the floor toward the grandma, asleep in her arm chair, a kitten rolled up beside it. A child is playing on the floor. I touch its soft hair. It is cold. An idea enters my mind. Have not all these been once alive, and now ice embalmed? I intrude no farther. None look up to ask me to stay. A charm comes over me driving all uncanny sense away. How pleasant to have our dead welcome among us, as though not lost.

Now I come to rooms of birds and other pets. A boa that swung Robet in olden time. What is this, an elephant like the mammoth, ice-locked in southern zone. Washed away?

"O auntie!"

I turn nervously around. It is not Miss Mae but Miss Serpenta. Show Off's betrothed, who has mistaken my name.

"Miss Robet is in the great hall, where Charley (mistake) is going to lecture. It is superbly decorated, a great globe of the earth in the center, colored. He will tell all about it. He has counted out a thousand and one inventions never seen here. He says he will lionize the natives. She told me to find you, for though any can enter an open archway, none can open a closed door."

I begin to feel as if Blue Beard lived here. The open rooms are so magnificent and shining one need not hunt him up.

"The cue in the halls," goes on the friendly girl, "is to keep on the smooth path. The lecture will soon begin. She is afraid you will take cold or something and wants you by to watch you."

"To watch me!" I muse maliciously. "Did I come, clear to Arc to be watched by an old maid, an old one truly?"

I turn to the rough path. What is that under that chair? I do believe it is a paper. Charley has dropped some of his notes. I am so tired. I will sit down while I pick them up. Why don't they come out? I get up and perceive the chair is an open work door, solid built.

"O," says Serpenta, trembling, as I hurry to undo the bar. She is paralyzed. As I open the door a little way, I see in the jar a Blue Beard. I said the lions are pink, this one is blue. His paw on the paper, his breath on me. No art manufacture now.

I dream in shadow. I see Show Off, who has followed his girl, with one tremendous blow put us two around an archway. The lions are in the room. They mind him not. When did a king mind? They see me not. I see them from reflections on the ice mirror walls.

He leans against a column and plays. (He has in his mouth a harmonica, Saucy's property.) Plaintive at first, then shrill, one note touches a chord in the lions' ears. They shake their heads. It comes again. They snort. A mother back of them calls to a lost babe; three heroes go to her aid flying. The door is shut. Tableau.

The lecture is very good. When it comes to lions I am surprised to see in the archway behind Charley, no less than Show Off astride his young thoroughbred, who, when lions are said to dance and play music in America, this one dances and plays behind the speaker, who looks back wild-eyed. The harmonica in its mouth, Show Off chokes out the strains with his hands. So apt and comical is it, the speaker himself breaks out laughing. Show Off has learned to read Unit writing. He got the paper under the door. Did not get left by a Unit scion.

I am sitting by the girl, who says:

"I could listen all day about the marvelous people when Aunt Robet takes you home I will go along."

"O say no more, I implore. I feel so lost when I think of home."

"To-morrow," I see she is going to make me happy again, "I will take you over the city. It is one of many that occur every ten miles. This side the river is our summer home, the other is our winter."

The next morning I take to the tower top and delight myself by discovering another motion still of the chairs. It is a circle whirl which I practice until I feel I am seasoned to any mode of motion sprung on me.

Serpenta seeks me out, and asks me sweetly what place we shall visit first.

"O, no matter."

"A library?"

"Very well."

She connects our chairs securely, as did Robet, and presses them to motion, without saying as did Robet, "look out."

We are moving—how, *how*? Her "look out," had she said it, would have helped one less than Robet's. For this is worse—so much more worse.

Not so exhilarating, quite the opposite. I am losing my breath in a faint, so utterly unprepared am I, for we are moving straight out into space. I look sideways to see Serpenta calm. I look in front, if to see a track, none there. Nothing above or below to hold, not even a wire. Still we are steady and aim to another tower top that is rapidly nearing. Now we stop on it. I get down and walk around my chair to find its wizard action. No track, did I say? There is a track—good rail track behind. It pops into my head it is after the method devised some years ago for a railroad to lay its track as it went, but must have land to lay it on. This carries and steadies its supplements—bridge-like.

We descend the elevator into an elegant room of many windows and drapery, seat ourselves beside one, high and wide. The scene outside is exquisite. Some fur-clad people are on the ice around a fire cooking. A ship in the distance is ice locked.

But there is no ice in this neighborhood.

"How do you like the picture?" asked Serpenta eagerly.

"O, the window is a picture; it is fine," I reply enlightened.

"Is it like your people that go in ships?"

"They must be the last explorers whom Savant found. How I wish I could rescue them and bring them into Arc."

"Did you say this is a library, where are the books?"

She presses on the picture frame; it changes as a part advances, opens and is a book. The back was part of the picture. It is Savant's story in pictured writing and quite enlists my sympathy. Seeing me tearful she takes me outside and leaves me in a shrubbery plot, while I attempt to compose my features.

Hearing a sob from someone else close by, I am upset again and weep in sympathy. I peer through the low-lying branches and see Robet in a mossy nook, giving way to hysterical bitterness, her hands over her face.

Now, two other hands pull them away to give her view of the laughing face of Show Off. She pushes him off spitefully. Partly losing his balance, he settles back on his heels, still laughing, seeing which with her toe she completes his overthrow and leaves him in the moss as she continues unconstrained her grief.

Show Off picks himself up sobered and looks around for other occupation. I do also view the surroundings. I perceive this building is over the river. Before I salute Robet, she arises and stamps away.

Passing my retreat I hear her moan:

"You are lost, O my darling."

Something drops gently upon my hand. I look down to see a round button-like object attached to a line that goes up above.

I raise it, when the string sways out from the tree, free from aught else but the sky.

I feel in my hand a signal, which I recognize. By my knowledge of Arc as a "hello," which I answer back. Then comes a communication:

"I am away up in the sky. Who are you?"

Thinking some trick is being played on me I answer:

"Robet."

Ting a ling ling. They are happy. (Can it be the Traveler?)

Hoping so, I telephone on the line, in Robet's voice:

"It is my darling!"

I hear back: "It is sounding from the clouds in accents of her voice. O, clouds, speak again."

"When will my darling come again?"

"Do you want me, dear? I will wander no more. But it is fine up here. I go like light. Thoughts cannot travel faster."

"My darling is like a spirit of air for speed."

"I will speed to you, dear."

"His daughter pines for him."

"Not her."

"My heart is full of love. This winter I will marry him and journey with him in the famous sky. Here are ten thousand kisses to last till winter shall bring him home."

"My coach frets to be going. But this winter it shall stop for a season."

The button darts upward.

Robet—I say in my mind—weep not. There are fairies around. I look up to see Show Off in front of me.

"What," he says, "come to school?"

"Yes," I answer vaguely, seeing no sign of such institution.

He slides back of me in the foliage, a door revealing a busy scene:

Men, women and children are scattered about, variously occupied. Some are writing upon sheets of transparent material. The pictured script, which subjected to a solution, is shrunk to microscopic dimensions. Other occupations are on each side, extending in a line.

On the farther side of each room are windows looking outside. The school rooms being divided from the inner halls and libraries by the umbrageous alley, in which we sit.

Wheeling my seat ahead (which goes, tree and all, as though one piece on rollers) Show Off explains:

"This school or fair, as Charley calls it, (would I could take it home for exhibition) is devoted to silk."

I see in process of construction pictures, screens, garments, carpets (which I had taken for sward) with American articles devised from Charley's lectures. These last are brought out to me for my benefit. A worker hands me a glass of water, which another puts a bouquet of flowers into, on which lights a canary and sings a song, as a fuzzy dog puts up his paws at my side. All are silk.

Down spinning comes a spider. I did not like its looks. It opens its mouth saying:

"Come into my parlor."

I turn away saying: "No American parlor this, but fairyland, sung of poets and imagined in spirit by painters. As I become absent-minded, Show Off closes the doors and leaves me alone."

I look straight up into the sky, thinking of the button, when an odd little sky speck attracts my inquisitiveness, for it is growing larger very last, as it no doubt is coming down very fast. Strangely heavy for a fleecy cloud, which it looks to be. Down to the opening, through to the tower top it stops by my side. The cloud is off, as out steps father and Saucy, and I spring convulsively to my feet off the rock I had leaned on in case.

Holding my hands together Mae quiets my nerves.

"O, auntie," with glowing cheeks and shining eyes of sky angel. "Did you not know they do this here? See, this is the string of the cloud balloon I hold."

"But Mae, the Traveler is up there and is not friendly."

"O, Grandpa has been civilizing him, so I have asked him to the wedding."

"How is that?"

"Serpenta is his niece, so he might as well come and be reconciled. Won't there be an explosive," she adds gleefully.

"Now Grandpa and Auntie," as she sits down by my side, "take up your bill of fare, and while we dine, we will talk of going home."

A table in our midst has been spread, a la American.

"Bill of fare?" I query.

"Yes, that menu by your plate."

I had taken it for a leaf decoration. It is named at the top *A Leaf From Webster*. Webster's dictionary? It is the first page of S as that initial heads each dish. Sabine-fish, sacar-game, saccharine-pastry, sack-drink.

Serpenta comes in with Show Off behind her and sits up opposite. As we part the fish with our knives and forks, so new to them, they are delighted and get us to do theirs.

As Saucy blandly puts a piece in her mouth with her fork, they rush to her, thinking her mouth speared. She drops the fork.

In father's hand is so familiar shape of white China cup and filling also. I hastily taste my own. It is "ice cream," the white cup a macaroon.

But as the spoon, with which I tasted, goes into my mouth, they rush to me, thinking it strained. We drop now our spoon and take up the sack, which is in Arc cups shaped like bottles, which are gum paste.

To cover our discomfiture, we arise in unison, touch and drink boon fashion. When boom, crack, roar, the ground beneath us shakes.

The two opposite, natives here, spring to their feet with distending eyes, standing transfixed as the cracking roar continues, listening to the approach of a sucking, whistling sound, which long drawn, lessens and gradually disappears when they recover composure.

My first idea of the panic was that it was God's displeasure of our dissipation. Quickly banishing this I recognized the crackling as that of ice, which denoted the real danger. The sucking sound was so like water, which, escaping to the river, had ended the commotion. Ah Arc! Highest of all! Yet is death ever beneath!

Resuming our seats I bethink me of Saucy's proposition:

"Going home, Saucy?"

"Yes, to America."

"To America!" I echo again.

"Yes, will this be an easy way?" getting up and coming to take hold of me, as though I was to be scared.

"An easy way." I cannot think what she is driving at, when it comes out.

"Yes, the way we are sailing in the air."

I clutch the rock (as did Fitz James) muttering as did he, "This rock shall fly from its firm base, as soon as I."

But too late, the rock is flying with me on it through the air in combination of the rest on the plot. Tower and schools are left behind, so quick done I had been unobservant.

By effort accepting the situation, I turn to Show Off, jocularly:

"How far can this go?" in reference to the proposition.

"To the sun, if you want a scorcher," he answers with assurance.

"I have been studying, Auntie." She studying, "We can place relays of these over the border."

"But the compass?" I interrupt.

"We will measure straight between each relay until the compass rights itself," sitting down herself contentedly.

I get up and choke her with a hug. "You blessed child, given me a way to get home."

I forgive her immediately and all the rest for the dreadful scares I have been victim. I think of home scenes, so far away, and compare with these of this delightful land. I must confess, I prefer as magnificence, these. But the blessed mascot has studied how to get home.

It being possible, my full spirits rebound.

"Next spring will do to go," I say, anxious now to stay, where before I was anxious to go—now that I could.

The next day I am so light of heart and light of step, I take trust that my old statue heaviness cannot again weigh me down.

Initiated to the schools, as the place where all work, (Arc life above, mostly a recreation) I become alert to choose an industry. Saucy arriving, takes from her pocket silk and needle, deftly fashions a butterfly, which she affixes, waving to my shoulder. As I ask: "What can I do?"

"O, you can print the books you write, you know. And Charley," laughing, "can paint."

The days fly swiftly by. The sun has rounded down toward the horizon. Twilight is our only day. Clouds skim the blue sky. Cream foam in portend of storm, driving us to the warmth of the towers that are now getting a layer of arctic protection.

Bright days only let us out to tour the cities, making the round trip roundly. Each tour develops a new specialty, marvelous and absorbing our interest. Though the upper sky, out of the crevasse, is getting a soft black color, still the air around has a light of its own that is not artificial in any sense—proceeding from the center aurora, that is becoming oftener in action. Scanning it closely one day, as I am returning home, I mistake the door and curiously look around at the grand hall in which I find myself.

The walls, like all others, shining and sparkling, are here, strangely glimmering and glinting, quite dazing my eyes.

I ask a slim little Arc maid I see walking about in absorbed fashion, "What place is this?"

"Holy Hall," is her impressive reply.

"Then you have a church after all. Do you pray to God?"

"Not in words as you. God knows before."

"Then what is Holy Hall?" I persist.

"Where people are holy."

"O, what makes it glisten so?"

"It holy spiritualizes all within."

"Then no evil spirits can come to this communion of saints." Quite bestows comfort and relief.

The walls are landscaped in crackled scenery, and at intervals against their centers aloft, are fastened most gorgeous state chairs, supported by brackets that have a separate and more distinct gleam. I turn again quickly, awed to inquire. I look into the face of Savant, who is intently regarding my expression.

"The chairs," I say, "are they alive?"

"Yes," he replies, "to make the dead alive, who will come to sit in them."

"O, is this where Roban saw the scientific angel?"

I rigidly regard the one nearest to me to see it being occupied by a familiar face and form. (Familiar by engraving). "It is *George Washington.*"

A hand appears from the air, resting on his arm, which slowly materializes the form to which it is attached.

I open my mouth in awe, for I recognize again President Lincoln—the *martyr*, as joining him in touch appear his generals. My memory goes back to that struggle of civil strength, at the sight.

Then I strive to awaken myself, as though I must have fallen strangely asleep, scarcely believing the illusion before me.

Not crediting the tales of spiritualist societies, I cannot likewise discredit the Bible records. Knowing I have not, as likely the excellent souls in Arc, have not, in wantonness profanely tempted this array, I, in deference to the manifestation, wait resignedly. I clasp my hands in added awe as Savant touches me to inquire:

"Who are they?"

"Upon the other side of our country's father has appeared. Ah, who? Jefferson Davis and his gray-clad staff."

I wring my hands as Savant touches me again.

"There was a war," I gasp. "Do they hear? They look down and smile at me, even the rebel, at whom I shake my finger."

"You caused it, to be a President. You tried to cut a great country in two; deluging it in blood."

In my electric state I see the root of the real cause—ambition of earthly state. The root of evil that grew to a tree of distrust of brother to brother. Each aroused in strength of pride to combat of their separate interests.

He replies resignedly. "I did not want war. It conquered back the Union."

The father hastily spreads his hands in benediction. So like prayer I ask:

"Do *you* go to *see God* in *spirit* form?"

Then dropping on my knees, "O tell me of Jesus."

"It was my republic. The kingdom of God to men—the people. He taught to pray for."

"How could you be 'Our Father' before you were born?"

"The testimony of Jesus is the spirit of prophecy."

"You, the Father of Jesus, how is He the son of God?"

"As such to teach republic love. I will ask my pastor."

"Will He come at the end of the second millennium in body form and bestow body life on good spirits to that end preserved?" I, endeavoring to prophecy.

"It will be evolved scientifically to all," astounds me.

"Good and bad, where will be room for them?" skeptic.

"Some will dwell in air; O, in cloud balloons."

"Will they eat and work as they do now?"

"The same."

"Must they live and cannot die?"

"Live or die as they do choose?"

"Have war?"

"There will be universal peace in a universal republic," as one foot steps forward to disappear.

I hurry to ask: "Was Jesus the Christ of the Jews?"

"The seed of Abraham in which all nations should be blessed."

"What about David's throne?"

"The promise was to Abraham, not to David. The latter's throne will be raised to a republic."

"Was the spirit of republic first of Jesus?"

"From the beginning of God."

As a foot disappears. "Will woman equalize in its rule, Presidentess as of God?"

"That is the universal rule."

Another foot starts, I haste again. "Who is the devil?" But he is gone too quick. And around about me come living people; friends at home.

"Can the living come?" I ask Savant, who is still near.

"In spirit form just the same."

I talk to them; they to me, the news of each. We walk about and discuss the people and the occasion, quite content in each other's society.

In the center of the room, upon a pedestal are Serpenta and Show Off. I do believe they have been married, for this has been the assembly. We arrive at their side with loving wishes, in time to see a chamois garlanded close by. We hear the word "initiation" and stuff our mouths at its American misapplication.

The crowd are gone and spirit friends. I say to Saucy:

"Let's go to bed," who replies:

"I have just woke up. I went in dream to see Mamma. She was crying. I put my arm around her neck and she leaned her head on me and was comforted. I told her I would come home in a cloud, which scared her so, I laughed out loud. She heard, and looked about the room, then took her work. I think I will go every night to see her."

My father is brushing by my arm. I say:

"O, what do you think, I saw my little children who are dead, in dear mother's care. They have been growing by my side. I knew them plainly and realize I have oft consciously caressed them. What is the element producing the phenomena?"

"It is positive electricity confined by glass. The balloons of clouds are thus manipulated and strong to carry a number of people. I am studying how constructed, to use them in our return."

I go out hastily into the night, the long night of this city. My mind so wrought upon by home people I look up at the velvet black sky, and pray:

> Silent night! Above me
> Thy sublimity far reaching
> Opens to Omniscience!
> Specks are thy sun system
> In dotted plain!
> Mindful of human pain—
> Communest thou peace?
> Longing to leave this place.
> Great everywhere, guide me,
> Guiding me here, guide me hence.
> I await thy signal
> In calm acceptance.

What? A Crown of Radiance arisen there. A solemn bell tolls forth; streams of light are shed around in spectrum sparks; the river banks are deserted; the towers tenantless, as each citizen hastens to the inner aisles of verdure depths, where issues shadowed fire.

I keep pace with Savant, whom first I see and reach with him an inner balcony that is endless in curving ring each side, making amphitheater around the city. The center is a great open rotunda, of fields, miles broad, of shaking ice. A flame of gold supplying the Crown above ascends out of a round cavernous crater in the center.

Savant seats himself on a raised broad platform, commanding a view of the whole scene. I unconsciously sit beside him. Beneath our feet I see a rug of "hel"iotrope. (NOTE. The quotation marks in the flowers give a double meaning. A "hel" meaning heel on the rug.) A hedge of "wall"flower hems us in from a row of poplar tree columns. Before us on a table is spread a set of "China" asters under a canopy of blue iris (flag). As Canterbury "bells" ring forth, we begin a feast.

The centerpiece is a large "sweet-pea"cock, flanked by "chick"weed on each side, "butter"cup, "pica"lily and "pitcher"plant have places.

Alarm at my heart at the solemn tolling bell had hastened my feet hither. To find a scenic banquet is somewhat puzzling. The usual ascending glow, with its usual reversal of shadows, is augmented by the added source, in new portraiture, adding to the picturesqueness of the occasion. Taught at home that all people without Christ are barbaric, I was expecting an abject worship of the disturbed elements. Instead I am pleased as surprised to find it an inspiration of interest only.

I look to get their knowledge of the phenomena. For its solution I have left home and risked my life. That they fear it not, is evident. Instead they love and reverence its benefaction to them—lighting and warming their homes all winter; their winter daylight—as Roban said, in their interior winter quarters. Unusually quiet this season so far, but this is to outdo all, make up for lost time, unprecedented in grandeur. That they understand it I am solicitous to know. I could catch a word now and then. I could understand in the voluble tonic, stream of talk I read from their gestures and expressive faces some meaning of their patriotic interest.

The morning banquet at an end, all sit back in their seats and look at Savant as though some special ceremony is to ensue. Thoroughly excited, I see him hold a state book and read:

"We receive again God's sign of the disturbance of aurora—our beautiful mother in the earth—who gathers us each winter around her fireside to comfort us in its warm beams."

"What is aurora?"

"Yearly we ask this question. None have answered us. We yearly invite our subjects to explore her confines, whence she lights her beacon. We invite now."

"Who will descend the Glory Hall to pay devoirs to the country's goddess."

I had followed him quite plainly. When he stopped, in the silence that followed a great light filled my eyes, as the idea that engendered it filled my mind.

I a"rose" in my seat, which latter is a rose vine—insignia of aurora—which word I hear in suppressed intuition in application to myself as a branch of bloom settles on my head wreath-like. Raising my hands in acceptance of the undertaking, they look calmly at me, incredulous, when I speak in full earnest tones:

"I will go, God of the universe, Creator of aurora has led me hither for that purpose."

Sitting again, they are convinced, and much upset in their calculations, that I so small should answer the great request.

In their surprise I get full revenge of all I have been subject of so long.

Now, all look at Savant, which occasions me to do the same. The phenomenal wave of thought, individual to him, wraps his countenance in stormy struggle. He speaks:

"We cannot accept, in duty to guest and stranger." But I gesture firmly.

Again he is submerged with greater struggles to exhaustion of his great strength, when an enduring calm arises in his face, like a smiling island in a hurricane tossed sea. Waving his hands, as I had done, he speaks:

"I will take you."

All arise in consternation and press about us. Mae, wild-eyed, shakes me back and forth. Father buries his face in his hands. Roba and Charley only, clap their hands. The tide now turns in our favor; all is pleasant bustle. The tender social visiting of their usual tenor and normal habit is changed to agitation in concocting a mode of preparation to ensure our safety, resulting in an elaborate scheme of training, to which we are subjected, separately, next day.

Bandaged securely we are rolled about and tossed. Suspended to a long rope we are dangled in mid air, swung in a circle with increasing speed. Hands are waved before us, jumping and shouting indulged in to harden our nerves. Left alone, click, the floor beneath is loosening, revolving, opening, black darkness ensues, then lights glimmer around; bells, whistles and reverberations fill all the air with din, followed by melody so low as scarcely to be heard—the music of the spheres.

This has taken days, as it has been necessary to repeat each lesson, over and over. Quite unnecessary, I think, is so much pains of preparation.

But at last the day is appointed, as all things are ready.

The city is astir from center to circumference. We are on view in Central Hall. The masses pass by us in solemn file to take leave of us, as of their dead. I feel to smile, but like the dead am turned to stone.

We next are placed in a round crystal globe receptacle. Packed in, Savant's unique instruments to his hand. Fluid food to our mouths through a tube. Condensed air to our nostrils. We are locked in by Savant.

Now carried out on a long platform pier toward the abyss and placed upon the top of a huge iceberg mass—as weight to sink us.

Dynamite hurls us out over fields and blocks of surging ice, lifting us into the rose enfolding pit. My sole experience is precipitation. Conscious of swift descent, unattended by jar, thrilled to the center of my being, I realize my position.

Readers, what is to ensue, is the special key to the phenomena of Astronomy. For the contents of the next few pages, I have written this story.

I am not the first who has thought the earth to be hollow, and entered at the Arctics. Also that a rolling fire, and open sea, are within. That I *define* this fire, and its *safe control*, thereby discovering the *secret* of our planet, and its object in the solar system, is the first time such definition has been given ever. Is of such high importance I deem it my solemn duty to publish it.

Adding a relevant definition of the Sun, and other sky objects, is but following out the line, struck by the first keynote.

In comparison with the present indefinite theory, this illustration far exceeds it in practical demonstration—ever satisfactory to truthful students.

Shelly in the time of Byron voiced this promise of the Arctics.

Poets have sung of its unknown city.

Capital and life have ever embarked for its discovery.

The smoke has cleared, leaving a steady moonlight, brightness intensified. I think to look below and see there a moon, round and glistening, many miles in width, its grandeur startling. Transfixed, I see it grow, as it is plainly coming up higher. To relieve my eyes I look to one side to see its appurtenances, only to find none. The sides of the cavern are far away and undiscernible. I am puzzled. Resolving to understand this unexpected bearing, I look first at my watch. A new puzzle is on its face. Its calendar declares the passage of days since I have been here. I turn square to the beautiful moon beneath me and bravely steady my understanding, for a queer unrest sensation is trying to creep on me.

Though I throw it off, in its terrifying aspect, yet it wraps me round and permeates my consciousness. That this moon, now so quiet and glittering, is not only the fire producing the Aurora smoke, but something more. The painful solicitude of Arc people at letting me do this daring act, that to me looked like mockery, is demonstrative of their better understanding. If Savant knew what was to happen, I cannot say, for I cannot speak to him, nor he to me, nor see each other's faces. I am alone with the problem I have put myself in. My old statue sense upholds me. I lean on it as I place straight the lines of new knowledge—that the moon I see is not a moon, but the central fire of the whole earth—the molten mass of astronomical science.

That it does not fill the whole center is second new knowledge, for a haze of distance is each side and above, denoting far removal of the earth-crust, egg shell, undiscoverable even by the powerful lens of the crystal globe around me. Central of the earth, it may be thousands of miles below, though slowly growing. My strained eyes take its impress on their inner orbs. Wherever I look it is there. I settle bravely to scan it, enchanted. A new phase comes over it. A flame column is rearing; breaks and sparks fly upward as coals snap outward. Should the latter hit the crust, so far away, it would stir it somewhat, giving the outward inhabitants a shock of earthquake. I have it—this is the cause of earthquakes. Third new knowledge.

Nearer to the flame that now rolls back and forth as if to engulf us, it bends downward on each side as if the space around it were also below it. Thus have I seen our hall lamp do at home when disturbed by air currents.

Lamp! Lamp! Is the earth a lamp?

Before me is the key note.

Hiss, crack! It is our life preserver—the iceberg beneath us. Melted to vapor it will ascend and carry our globe to Arc again.

Listening with wildly beating heart in intense suspense, I become unconscious as fiery serpents twine beneath me.

At last recovered I look again; but no longer there. Ah, above? Have we passed it?

Below it and still descending. I lean heavily and wholly on my statue. The days make no impress on me. Not even when I see the sky out of southern zone. Coldly viewing the Southern Cross Constellation of sun stars, the planet Mercury comes between, taking on a peculiar distinct phase. I sluggishly remember that in a mine the planets are seen thus at noon-day. Ah! is the earth's center to be a mine to me?

My eyes become exhilarant as I quickly investigate. I can see its (Mercury's) rivers, mountains plainly. I can see into it. As I get excited, I see an inside flaming fire, as earth's. Then it is—yes, a lamp, also.

The planets lamps? Where are their chimneys? I inspect again. There certainly is no chimney to guard the draught. I will study. Oh, why did I not notice before, it is more like a Chinese lantern—candle inside, colored shade outside.

I look in ecstasy for days. It is, as is our dear mother earth, a beautiful Japanese lantern; made by Deity's hand to revolve around the glowing sun.

A sun ray spectrums the interior of earth. O, beam alive with electric, spirit intelligence, give me a sign. The sun itself comes. My eye, on fire, looks into its soul. O, sun, what art thou? Worshiped by some as God, by all as a great life giver. Ages past and future will you roll, unguided by man.

I am now so hot I wonder if I have partly warmed the inside of my statue being, (so wholly benumbed I became at the knowledge of passing below the earth's center, inside light—losing all shadow of hope of seeing Arc again—that my marble state was more than ever marbleized). Now that I am treated, in lieu of home, to new explanations of past astronomical phenomena, is some recompense to my constitutionally enthusiastic mind.

Holding down an equally strong impulse to desire to tell this new acquisition, I let it unfold to myself to warm me under my marble shield. What follows fast? Vision upon vision is enlarging my interior sense of human life, until my outside is only cold. My whole inner is seething in ardor until my eyes break through the statue thrall. Too hasty—the light blinds me. I close them impatiently; open slowly.

Is the sun a China lamp? O, no, no; but an American electric arc light. I hurrah unrestrainedly!

Around it dance its gay planets as it sits and beams warmly upon their atlas garniture—a round crystal-globed lamp. I see a marking on the disc. Does it designate a disturbance within? It grows and changes. Would that some astronomer were here. The globe in which I sit is steady in its motion, but the marking on the sun changes oft. I look up toward the earth flame to see coming from its side more coals and smoke; also so far one side as to clear its blaze safely, is a huge mass—yes, ice—coming swiftly directly over me. Having collected all this hard winter, it has rolled over the edge of Arc to complete my destruction for my daring temerity. Resolving to retain consciousness, I look downward at the sun spot. It has changed; is changing, as does the ice-mass above me. Can that mass, in eclipse from the light above, be the spot? I believe it is, and that it will now strike us.

Hitting only on the edge of our anchor, ice, it spins the globe off into space, over and over, vapor spouts adhering. But I have seen behind us a slim stationary object. Is it? Oh, is it a fixture to hold the earth flame?

Relieved of our heavy ice we gravitate to it (as the ice-mass evaporates, filling the interior with Aurora prisms. These escaping at both northern and southern zone outlet, are certain proof of the attending phenomena).

Sliding along its length we curve toward the side of the earth which I shall hope soon to see. Coming at last far away, like a cloud, now to it, we dip down (or the rod fixture on which we slide, as though some inner electric lode drew us).

This quite mysterious direction engages my study as we pass under the earth-crust, as it, China-lantern transparent like, curves by above us as if in a rim. I study; why the crust of the earth turns round and round, and not the rod! Surely no earthly lantern is so elaborately constructed.

Engaged in study I find myself outside. The rod arises now in height of location and branches to each side of the crust-rim, fork like. Extending, we go out, out toward the sun. As we lightly bound hither and thither, side and about, I catch a backward glance of the continent America. Tears fill my eyes. As I press them out I see approaching a white cliff on the rod, covering its width. This side are crowding a swarm of tiny people absorbed in dislodging a huge boulder of which the ground is covered. Clinging about them is a semi-transparent vapor that floats and densifies, collecting over their heads. They jump into the air, whirl over harlequin like and descend to push again the boulder.

No sign of vegetation; there must be no air. Can the vapor be their breath? Why does it not float away? In the globe I have tubes to my nose that supply my breath.

The little fairies, are they (I pinch myself) getting into mischief? An adult makes peace by administering sharp pinches. As one moves its mouth to howl, I do too, but cannot make a sound; neither does the child who cries without. I see the reason. A thin filmy gauze surrounds it confining the vapor breath.

Over goes the boulder lightly as if hollow. Losing its rod gravitation it flies off toward the earth and disappears (dashing on its surface—an aerolite).

Ere they select another we enter their midst. Not seeing us within, they grasp the globe and roll it over. Seeing a debris marring its shining surface they pound it off. This removed from the fastening Savant swings it open, Pandora-box-like, as off they rush. Winding carefully his breath tubes about him, Savant takes tools, solutions, etc., and stepping out carefully inspects the boulder's surface. (Are they the dust on the rod?) Selecting one he quickly works. Indents and excavates a large round cavity, disclosing a glittering black diamond interior, disappearing inside as he works. I, curiously steer the globe to the entrance. The inside smooth he places a block in the center, obvious as rest to the globe which I steer to and stop on, seeing myself an equal distance from the interior sides. Satisfied, he proceeds to throw a solution over the latter, which brings out a picture or reflection from the globe-disc, camera-like. Is the picture the interior of the earth? I scan it curiously.

After the ice border (around the north pole) land with one only vegetation, a white cactus. White is the color of the whole inside except some blackened spots. The cactus skin is clothing of a people who appear, who eat the pulp and work the thorns into houses and into ships as water, first shallow, deeper grows; and again into forts upon the cacti brunches growing up out of the water, thorn protected from sea monsters. Then these last range alone.

A great blur where we passed the light, more sea includes the lower half.

I exclaim to myself in bitter mood, is this all!

I am quite disenchanted. Is this our brother earth man? So flat; more wide than tall, who cannot lift his feet on account of his centrifugal location; thorn artists; skewering hair, umbrella like. Nesting on trees as high as Jack's beanstalk. A shade outside draws us hastily there. How came this emerald lawn with ruby roses, sapphire lilies, made of the gem rock centers.

The shade increasing relieves my eyes to see distinctly. As the tiny artists finish their work by sprinkling the sparkling dust over themselves and resume their jubilee racket. Suddenly I get an odd sense that they are different from ordinary human beings. Grace in every motion. Fair flowing hair; deep-dell gray eyes are of plain human being species. Still I notice strongly a difference as they gather now and hurriedly consult. Children and adults. Are the latter all mothers or fathers? I cannot tell.

Before solution dawns I look up and find the moon is approaching close over. Is it whence the unique mites have their origin?

Still in the globe, my attention turns wholly to it, for the globe-lense shows it distinctly enough to read its surface. Its mountains, valleys, and—yes, certainly, human cities grow upon my vision. So interested am I, I forget to look for appurtenances or attachment fixtures, in my new custom of practical demonstration.

As I get an important discovery of inventive construction in a certain locality straight in my mind, it is almost knocked out, as now, directly over, I perceive a central light inside the satellite. It is a taper-kind and in disturbance. A burst of blackness drops from it and down toward me. Keenly alarmed, the tots are more so, as they, run and fall down and dig faces and hands beneath the boulder debris.

As trembling thus they lay, I get another impress of them which suddenly takes definite form. The solution is present. The father and mother, before mysterious, are also present. What is quite astonishing, these two are one human being. Uncanny sense gives way to delight at the vision of strength and dignity, so masculine; enhanced by grace and tenderness, so feminine.

I feel to clap my hands, but the inky blackness is coming down so fast I look to it. Wavering white spots are on it; reflections of the white cliffs below. The forks of the rod are plain and take on a familiar contour. Contour of the Milky Way. Is *that* a mirage of this rod on night sky?

The cloud falls and fells Savant too, nearly breaking the globe, as it splashes upon the nearest white cliff. The air now clears and cools as the deposit whitens, emitting a familiar odor. What! wax dropped out of the moon?

The tots arise and fly with gauzy robes to the cliffside and clamber excitedly about. Savant arises and enters the globe, proceeding to steer that way.

As the moon takes a smiling adieu I turn my attention again to it. I hunt some before I find a faint line, far away attached to the earth-rim, obviously its fixture. Simple but inexplicable in action. Though an electric connection in the rim may turn the earth-crust it would not also turn the moon, as the latter's motion is monthly, not daily.

Unable to solve this I complete my former broken discovery that the constructions on it are telescopes. Mining, maybe. Informing its people of the earth and how to get there.

Approaching the cliff a digging is heard inside. Then breaks out a waxen aperture, (closed by the splash) and out peeps a tiny head. We follow the rest, unseen, into the inner court of their mountain lodge.

Wax-carved alcoves, cloud styles, line a large area open in the center thinly to the sky. In one a tiny table holds tiny plates of brittle make. In them, what? A giant mosquito trapped in the outer wax, its denuded wings wrapping the imp robbers. Another alcove in high cloud has a choir, lace draped and seated. I recollect the mist people.

In the center of the sward plaza, or esplanade, is a circular fountain, enclosing within its circular wall of water a dell or green glen. Covering our top, we steer through the fountain side and to it. Discovering ourselves to the others, who scurry angrily behind us, we descend the dell, sloping down like a funnel, to find it shortly cut off. But lower down—ground again. While gazing at the latter a sensation strangely affects me, that it is moving——moving slowly by.

What is it? In the fixture—lubricated by the fountain in each white cliff (cooling the wax), moving as does the earth-crust. We are both lost in study.

The tiny fiends' anger culminates, as altogether they give the globe a sudden push. That taking Savant unawares, it is precipitated through the funnel and to the moving ground below. Electric tremors shake us up, but, insulated, our globe survives, and passes on the ground motor out of sight of the enemies above. A signal from Savant, but e'er I look ahead, a cake of wax drops upon my lap. I look up and see the wee gnomes above, clinging like fireflies to the ceiling. Their fun is shortened, though, as one accidentally, also drops, landing safely in the cake of wax. Zip, down comes a gauze ribbon, up which goes the little gnome too frightened to fly.

Breaking up the cake, I see in it a mould of the harlequin form, which I proceed to restore and dress, to his consternation. My attention thus diverted sideways is attracted by the width of the cavern. The cause soon obvious. It contains other motor ground beds. The twin of this on which we lazily ride is close by, but moving in an opposite direction, like a band reaching out and returning. Does it contact with the earth-crust, and turn it in daily curve? Then what do two others, on each side of these, farther out, but opposite, also, and smaller in size, turn—more slowly turn? Is it the band of the fixture of the moon, *attached to the earth-crust rim*?

I now look ahead—in my head—a sun—earth and moon. What next?

The tube "O! O!" is a telescope: greater than that of earth center; as so much longer. Shall I see God?

No, only a comet! "What art thou—a sky steamboat, or a torch flambeau? If the latter, then is the universe a *campaign, illumination, ratification*? And hast thou a human hearer on mighty sidereal parade?"

A living being is by it. (Oh, only a babe chub swinging in the tube.)

It is gone, and we too are going out.

Globe protected from the dazzling light, we look around and see a slow-going meteor—the rest had flew so fast, we had not time to read them.

This is so like our globe in which we ride. I cry, "Is *this* a sky meteor? This our globe?"

Answering not, Savant claps his bands, a reverberating crackling following. The other slops and turns our way. In it, as Engineer, sits the Traveler, at whom I will scowl no more, for by his side is Robet, in bridal phase.

Wuu, wu, w— —

"What big, round eyes."

I look around me, as I lay in my hammock on my little porch. Directly in front of me is Saucy, a grown-up young lady, as genial and ingenuous as ever.

"Now you are really awake, I will tell you what you have been doing while you were asleep. When I found you here and began slowly swinging you, you sang out: 'Give me a butterfly's wing.'"

When I fanned you, you groaned, "Lost, lost, oh, the ice."

"Then Charley came." (I see him, laughing behind a vine); "then talked gibberish to you, to see if you were asleep. You commenced making signs with your hands. Then slept soundly for a long time.

"Getting restless you held to the hammock sides, as if you felt to be falling.

"A branch of wistaria brushing your cheek, you grasped and began eating it. So I laid a banana on your hand, which you threw off as if it were a snake and bit you. Bernard (the dog) licked your hand, when you fainted clear away. To restore you, we shook the hammock. You then made your feet go as in dancing, ending as in prayer.

"Then you opened your eyes and looked straight ahead for a long time. Charley got a glass of water and sprinkled your face. Dropping the glass on the stand, you spoke in absorbed fashion, 'Meteor,' then awoke."

*   *   *   *   *

A dream! Only a dream! It was more—it was a grand inspiration. I will write it all down.

The beautiful coach, with sail wings, the sea and ice tour. The city of Arc, city of Zion! The marvels of perpetual amusements, science and spiritism—of God(?).

Going down the earth's center—the awed terror. Seeing into the planets—I did, too, I know I did.

I will write it all out.

I have spoken aloud my dream, to two very intent listeners, one of whom is convulsed anew. "A China-lantern" — will he never stop laughing. The other, "all right, auntie. You have got it right, and, if I mistake not, some other things. Though seen in a dream, it is not the less valuable tour, sought for ages. But the ancients did not have arc-light suns, to see their lanterns by, as do we. But why is the decoration set so far apart, unlike ours, that are close lantern-hung?"

"Oh, I can answer that," says Charley. "The design is but in outline. We will some day catch a meteor, and go to inspect it closer."

Lector House believes that a society develops through a two-fold approach of continuous learning and adaptation, which is derived from the study of classic literary works spread across the historic timeline of literature records. Therefore, we aim at reviving, repairing and redeveloping all those inaccessible or damaged but historically as well as culturally important literature across subjects so that the future generations may have an opportunity to study and learn from past works to embark upon a journey of creating a better future.

This book is a result of an effort made by Lector House towards making a contribution to the preservation and repair of original ancient works which might hold historical significance to the approach of continuous learning across subjects.

HAPPY READING & LEARNING!

LECTOR HOUSE LLP
E-MAIL: lectorpublishing@gmail.com

9 789354 206436